ESCAPE FROM A VIDEO GAME

THE ENDGAME

DUSTIN BRADY

ILLUSTRATIONS BY JESSE BRADY

Andrews McMeel
PUBLISHING®

Other Books
by Dustin Brady

Introduction

WARNING. This book is dangerous. And not just papercut dangerous. More like permanent-imprisonment-inside-of-a-video-game dangerous. Stay safe by following these steps:

1. Only turn to pages you're instructed to in boxes that look like this:

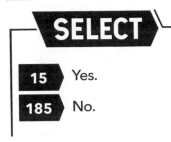

If you read the book in order, bad things will happen. What kind of things? Just ask Bryce Dillington of Port Matilda, Pennsylvania. Um, actually, wait. Our lawyers are saying that they very much don't want people talking to Bryce. OK, never mind. Just don't be like Bryce.

2. If you get confused by any of the puzzles or instructions in this book, check the hints and solutions section in the back. If you're still confused, write the author at dustin@dustinbradybooks.com and kindly suggest that he STOP MAKING SUCH COMPLICATED PUZZLES! THESE ARE KIDS' BOOKS, FOR CRYING OUT LOUD!

3. Don't fret if you die. It's a video game! No one really dies in a video game. Simply follow the checkpoint to return to your last saved location. Wow, that was nice of the author to include checkpoints! Don't you feel bad about that mean email you just sent him?

RETURN TO CHECKPOINT ON P. 53

4. Feel free to write in this book unless it's a library copy. In that case, please compliment your librarians on their taste in books and visit escapefromavideogame.com to print a worksheet you can write on instead.

5. Every section in this book starts with a grid that looks like this:

These grids will become important later in the story. Until then, feel free to use them as patterns for your quilting project.

6. Every section in this book ends with a secret letter that looks like this:

What are the letters for? OK, literally two sentences earlier, you read that it's a secret! You're going to need to pay closer attention if you want to survive this book. Be patient, and you'll learn the secret of the letters at the end of the book. Oh, also . . .

7. Don't skip to the end of the book like Zuzu Natson of Cedar Falls, Iowa. Poor Zuzu.

GRIM ISLAND

Drop. Destroy.
DOMINATE.

CHOOSE YOUR DESTINATION

(A) **Creepy Country**

(B) **Museum of Villainous Excellence**

(C) **Chaos City**

(D) **Azkaar Asylum**

(E) **Endgame**

(F) **???**

(G) **Boom-Boom's Adventure Zone**

(H) **Grim Energy**

(I) **Dreadful Dump**

(J) **Apex Airport**

Meet the Team

ALPHA

BONZAI

CHAZ

DARK PULSE

MISS ELEANOR

The Adventure Begins

HERE ARE ALL OF THE THINGS that are good about shopping malls:

1. Escalators

2. Food court samples

3. Pet store puppies

That's it. That's the entire list. Malls are for back-to-school shopping and waiting outside of changing rooms and detours into the candle store when your mom spots signs for their semiannual sale. Nothing exciting ever happens at the mall.

Until today.

The fateful moment happens just outside Moonicorn, a store that exclusively sells bedazzled T-shirts. (That last detail's not important to the story; you just need to understand why Moonicorn will be out of business within three months.) There's a commotion behind you. You spin to see a woman in a brown leather jacket running your way. At first, you guess that she's late for her shift at Moonicorn. She certainly looks like the type of young college student who works the register in those kinds of stores. But she's not running like she's late. She's running like she's on a mission.

You try stepping out of her way, but she moves in the same direction as you. You duck left, and she mirrors that motion too. You hold up your bag of back-to-school khakis as a shield, and she barrels right into it.

Your head smacks against the marble floor. You see stars. Then, the mystery woman leans close to your ear and whispers two words:

"Pay attention."

Wait, what?! You stumble to your feet, but she's back up and running. A salesman at the perfume kiosk tries stopping her, perhaps to be a hero, but probably to offer a sample spritz. Mystery Woman's not interested in perfume. Instead, she does something that shocks the entire mall.

She spins around the perfume salesman, jumps a railing, then dives headfirst into the lower-level mall fountain.

Mall fountains, if you're not aware, exist entirely to tempt people to throw in pennies. Fountain pennies account for half of most malls' income. Because these coins are so valuable, malls fill their fountains to a precise depth that allows people to see the pennies they've thrown, while keeping the pennies just out of reach of preschoolers' stubby arms.

All that to say, you would never survive a headfirst dive into a mall fountain.

But the woman in the brown leather jacket doesn't die. She doesn't quite survive either. Right before hitting the water, she vanishes with no flash, no poof, and no explanation.

Someone screams in horror. Someone else claps as if she's just seen a magic trick. A bunch more people pull out their phones, even though there's nothing left to film. A mall cop finally shows up and stares at the fountain with his hands on his hips. It's the most amazing thing that has ever happened at the mall.

Pay attention.

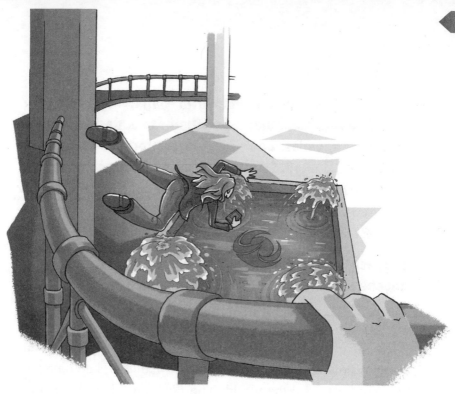

You rub your head and think about Mystery Woman's words. Pay attention to what? The dive? Are you supposed to figure out how she did it? You close your eyes and replay the scene in your mind. She was holding something, right? Like a phone, maybe? Were there any other clues?

Your mom interrupts your thoughts to make sure you haven't been permanently traumatized. You assure her that you're OK, but you wouldn't say no to a cinnamon pretzel. You get that pretzel from the food court, then head home.

That's when the real adventure starts.

You open the shopping bag in your bedroom and find this book. Um, you didn't buy a book. You slowly pull it out. It tingles in your hand. Is this from the woman in the leather jacket?

You read the back cover.

Greetings, villain.

Please accept this invitation to Grim Island, where you'll squad up with four other supervillains to outlast Earth's mightiest enemies. Don't get too comfortable around your allies, though. Survive to the Endgame, and you'll learn just how ruthless your teammates can be. One hundred villains will enter, but only one will be crowned Greatest Supervillain of All Time. Will it be you?

Experience Bionosoft's brand-new battle royale before anyone else. Bionosoft: Reality Reimagined.

Your heart starts racing. Bionosoft. The company that figured out how to put people into video games. The company that almost destroyed the world. The company that claimed to be out of business. Now, you're learning that they're not only very much in business but also testing brand-new games and catchy slogans.

You open this book and find a single choice: Accept the invitation?

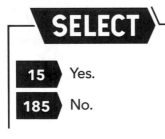

SELECT

15 Yes.

185 No.

WHEN YOU TOUCH THE "YES" BUTTON, you hear a *beep-beep-BEEP!*

On the third beep, you fall like you're on one of those amusement park rides that drops you straight down a tower. Those rides are the worst. They don't take you somewhere cool like a roller coaster or stick you to the wall like the Gravitron. No, your only reward for waiting in a one-hour line is three seconds of that unpleasant "oh no!" feeling in your belly.

"OH NO!" your belly screams when the book drops you down, down, down into darkness. Finally, you crash. Then you hear a voice.

"Alpha?" the voice whispers. "No wayyy. Guys, check this out! It's Alpha!"

You look for the voice's owner, but your world remains dark.

"Alpha's on our team!" the voice says louder.

"Chaz, be cool," someone else warns.

"WE HAVE ALPHAAAAA!" Chaz screams in a very uncool way.

You try rubbing your eyes, but your hand clunks into a helmet instead.

Zing!

Your visor powers up, and the world comes into focus. The name "CHAZ" floats above a lanky dweeb in rumpled army clothes. He looks like the default skin in a game that desperately wants its users to pay for an upgrade. Chaz is grinning stupidly and waving. "Hi, Mr. Alpha! Or Mrs. Alpha. Ms. Alpha? I don't want to presume. Allow me to be the first to welcome you to the team. We are the Bestie Boys!"

"GRR!" someone growls in protest. You glance over to find a green muscle monster who looks like Shrek's less attractive brother. Your helmet has labeled this ogre, "BONZAI."

"Bonzai, we've talked about this," Chaz explains. "We're all besties . . ."

"I'm no one's bestie," a female voice interjects.

"And I am sorry, sugar, but we are not boys," says yet another teammate.

You turn to find the two females in your squad. According to your visor, they're "DARK PULSE" and "MISS ELEANOR." Dark Pulse is a purple fox dressed in ninja garb. She probably weighs as much as one of Bonzai's forearms, but something about the way she carries herself makes you think that she'd hold her own in a fight against the big monster. Miss Eleanor, on the other hand, might be the least intimidating person you've ever met. She's from the 1800s or 1700s or whenever it was that people rode those bicycles with one giant wheel in front. She wears a hoop skirt, carries a Princess Peach umbrella, and wiggles her fingers at you in a coy little wave.

Chaz smiles. "Five best friends, ready to take on the world. So where are we dropping, Bestie Boys?"

"AHHHHHH!" Bonzai launches himself at Chaz.

This is all a bit much. Every member of your team feels like an over-the-top cartoon character. You just want a real person to help you with the 5,000 questions you now have.

While Bonzai wrestles Chaz, you check out the nearest reflective surface to figure out what you're supposed to be.

You raise an eyebrow when you finally see yourself. Now you know why Chaz was so excited to have you on the team. You're covered in sleek black armor, kind of like a Batman who has actual superpowers and doesn't need to dress like a tank to protect himself. You've got big muscles too. You flex and poke your bicep. Dark Pulse sidles up midpoke.

"First time?" the purple fox asks.

"Oh! Uh, yeah," you admit, a little embarrassed.

"It's a standard battle royale," Dark Pulse explains. "Twenty squads of supervillains get trapped together. They all find weapons and fight each other until one team is left standing."

You're in a bare metal box with two benches, a few backpacks, and one small window. There's barely room for one squad in here, let alone 20. Dark Pulse can tell what you're thinking, so she motions to a window.

Oh! Superbright. After your eyes adjust, you can see that you're actually in a military airplane flying over lava. Miles and miles of bubbling red lava. Is this the surface of the sun? Wait. No, there's an island up ahead.

"Grim Island," Dark Pulse explains. "Governments from around the world send their worst villains here. You can drop wherever you want, but I like the amusement park. Lots of loot and an easy path to the Endgame." She gives you a sideways glance. "Has anyone told you about the Endgame?"

"Uh . . ."

Dark Pulse flashes a smile that cartoon foxes make when they spot a chicken coop. She glances at the rest of the team. Bonzai is still fighting Chaz, and Miss Eleanor is staring into space while twirling her parasol. Dark Pulse lowers her voice. "We can't win with these guys. Why don't we ditch the team and do this on our own?"

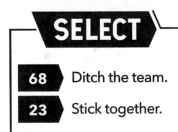

SELECT

68 Ditch the team.

23 Stick together.

THIS IS A VIDEO GAME, RIGHT? Video games have cheat codes. You've just got to figure it out. Unfortunately, you've never figured out a cheat code in your life. That's what YouTube is for.

You try pressing buttons on an imaginary controller. You yell, "Up, up, down, down, left, right, left, right, B, A, start!" to the sky.

Nothing works. Also, the game seems to be against you. Every time you pass up a weapon in search of an exploit, you get killed.

"I have a message for the game," you tell Bonzai in one particularly low moment. "I just want to cheat. Can you pass that along?"

Bonzai clunks you on the head.

S   **❗ ACHIEVEMENT UNLOCKED**
KONAMI CODE
RETURN TO CHECKPOINT ON P. 75

THE MUSEUM OF VILLAINOUS EXCELLENCE (MOVE for short) sits on 15 pristine acres near the center of Grim Island. It's got a lovely botanical garden, gargoyles galore, and a space for traveling exhibits. (A banner declares that this month's is "Mind Meld: Experience the Electrocution.") Oh, also, the museum has a spike trap at the entrance, so watch out.

After hurdling the spikes, you grab a lightning gun next to the ticket counter.

"Save your power!" Dark Pulse says as she runs toward the museum's grand staircase.

"Why?" you yell, but Dark Pulse has already passed you.

Chaz grabs your arm and leads you toward the stairs. "The traveling exhibit has a different superweapon every match that can only be activated by a certain type of superpower. This one is electric, so we need you."

"Fine, but why are we running?"

PEW!

That's why you're running. It's another squad, and they want the same thing you do. Your team dives into an alcove at the top of the stairs to dodge the laser blast.

PEW! PEW! PEW!

They're running up the stairs now. What do you do?

SELECT

42 Fight them yourself.

72 Send Chaz.

E	3	D
4	●	Y
7	S	V

DARK PULSE SMILES when she sees the jungle. She is deadly in the shadows. Your team hides under fake prehistoric leaves before the other squad rounds the corner. You try staying as still as possible, but there's a monstrous mechanical mosquito buzzing around the exhibit ("Nature's first villain!" a plaque boasts).

"Come out, come out, wherever you aaaare." Footsteps slowly walk past the exhibit. Hey, maybe they won't even find your team!

"ACHOO!"

Miss Eleanor breaks the silence with a dainty, yet surprisingly loud sneeze. The mosquito is resting on her upper lip.

The villains snicker as they enter the jungle. As soon as the last one steps into the exhibit, Dark Pulse gets to work. She's so stealthy that you don't even see her—you just hear the results of her work.

"AH!"

"Ooh!"

"Stop! STOP!"

"Yiiiiiipes!"

TURN TO

P. 143

❶ ACHIEVEMENT UNLOCKED
NATURE'S FIRST VILLAIN

YOU SHAKE YOUR HEAD. If only Dark Pulse knew how much you need the rest of your team to survive.

Miss Eleanor strolls over. "What are y'all darlings discussin'?"

"Alpha wanted to ditch you all," Dark Pulse says.

"What?! No, I didn't!" You are genuinely shocked by the betrayal of a fox who, just moments ago, tried to betray the rest of the team.

Dark Pulse smirks. "Said you were losers."

Miss Eleanor turns to you. She looks angrier. Scalier. "You think I'm a loser?!" she asks in a deep voice. You stammer an answer, but she won't listen. Instead, she grows a snout and sharp teeth. In a few short moments, she's transformed from a polite Southern belle into a crocodile in a dress.

You stumble backward when Miss Eleanor tries chomping your arm. When Chaz sees the confrontation, he squirms away from Bonzai to play peacekeeper. "I'm sure this is just a big misunderrrr . . ."

Miss Eleanor makes the misunderstanding even bigger by grabbing Chaz by the torso, kicking open the plane's back hatch, and throwing the Bestie Boys leader overboard. She turns back to you. You wrap your body around one of the backpacks on the wall, but Miss Eleanor is much stronger than you anticipated. She pulls both you and the backpack off the wall, then tosses you out of the plane.

You spot Chaz falling with his hands behind his head, eyes closed, and a goofy smile on his face. You dive to catch up. "WHAT ARE YOU DOING?!"

"I LIKE TO RELAX WHEN I GET THROWN OUT OF PLANES!"

"THIS HAPPENS A LOT?"

"KIND OF, YEAH." Chaz peeks over at you, then gasps. "YOU'VE GOT A PARACHUTE! PULL THE CORD!"

The backpack is a parachute! Of course. You strap it on, and Chaz holds tightly to your body. Finally, you pull the cord.

WHIP!

"Woohoo!" You cheer your good fortune just before smashing into a pile of garbage.

When you stagger to your feet, you realize that you and Chaz have landed at the Grim Island dump. The dump turns out to be both smellier and more popular than you would have imagined. Costumed villains are gliding in from every direction. There's a cowboy with an elaborate mustache to your right. A ballerina has landed on your left. A bear with a crown and monocle is digging through the trash above you.

And there's fighting. Lots of fighting. The ballerina blasts the cowboy with a small revolver that somehow produces a cannonball. Then, the bear takes her out with a gun that appears to shoot literal porcupines. Every eliminated fighter disappears in a cloud of blue smoke and gets tracked by a counter on your visor.

ENEMIES REMAINING: 95

94

93

You stumble around the dump, doing your best to avoid conflict. Where did Chaz go? Everything's so loud. Everyone's moving like they have a plan. Finally, you bump into your teammate.

"What do we do?!" you yell over the commotion.

"We loooooooot!" Chaz replies. He's gleefully picking up glowing objects that might be weapons but also might be radioactive trash. "The dump has loot you can't find anywhere else on the island! Ooh! Like this!" He holds up a bow and arrow that appears to have a dirty diaper on the tip. "Stink from the Sky!" He aims at a pirate with a robot parrot on his shoulder.

WHOOSH!

The diaper arrow zips 10 feet over the pirate's head.

"ARGH!" The pirate whips out an insanely huge hammer and lumbers toward you. He's way faster than you'd expect thanks to a spring-loaded peg leg.

Chaz runs right and points left. "EAT THAT!"

Eat what? The only thing you see is a can of garbage chili with a picture of the devil on it. Do you eat it?

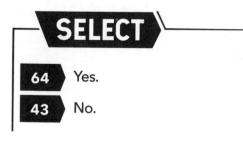

SELECT

64 Yes.

43 No.

"WHAT DID YOU DO?!" Dark Pulse shrieks when the bridge falls.

"Nothing!" Chaz yells. For once, this is actually true.

BANG!

Another team crashes through the door and takes out Dark Pulse. The rest of your squad scurries deeper into the fun house.

Looks like they're in the maze. Here's another opportunity to separate the squad. You turn off the lights.

"Great balls of fire! What now?" Miss Eleanor exclaims. All three teammates turn on flashlights. Miss Eleanor looks at her watch. "It says Alpha's right here in this maze."

You're actually above the maze, but they can't see that on the map. Now, that gives you an idea! You sneak down a trapdoor and creep through the maze.

> *Sneak up behind either Bonzai or Miss Eleanor. Figure out which one you can reach without getting spotted by a flashlight.*

SELECT

78 Bonzai.

69 Miss Eleanor.

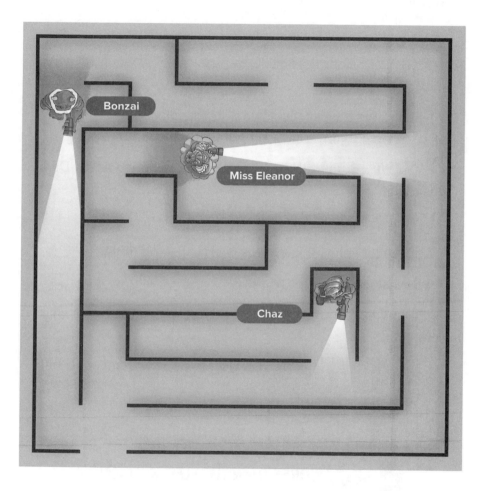

DARK PULSE LOOKS at her watch. "The zone is closing quick, so you have to figure this out in under a minute."

The Mind Meld is a tall throne with a glass dome suspended over it.

"Do I just sit in here?!" you yell.

"GRRR!" Bonzai points at a panel with a bunch of wires sticking out of it.

You run to the panel, and your heart sinks. You're supposed to zap it, aren't you? That's not going to happen.

"You used up all your electricity, didn't you?" Dark Pulse asks.

"Um . . ." You look at your hands.

"Even though you knew this was an electric thing."

Bonzai grunts his displeasure.

"But what about those mad-scientist weapons? Those were cool, right?"

No one has time to answer because you all fall into boiling lava.

E ❗ ACHIEVEMENT UNLOCKED
WORSE THAN THE ELECTRIC CHAIR

RETURN TO CHECKPOINT ON P. 72

```
B 5 D
K O 3
4 M I
```

YOU HOP TO YOUR FEET and run at the back wall. When you hit it, you don't bounce off, but you don't go straight through either. Instead, the wall stretches like it's elastic. You push and strain and finally pop through.

Now, you're in a hallway of nothingness. No floor, no walls, no ceiling. You move your legs, but it's impossible to tell if you're actually walking. Then you feel a tap on your shoulder.

"AH!"

You spin around and see the woman in the brown leather jacket. She tries to hug you. "You made it!"

You step back from the hug. "Who are you?"

"My name's Liz. I need your help."

"I'm just trying to get home."

"I know," Liz says. "The problem is, we're dealing with something big. Like fate-of-the-world big. So you need to help me first."

Is this part of the game, or is she for real?

"I'm going after this guy who calls himself 'the Builder,'" Liz says. "The only thing I know about him—the only thing anyone knows about him—is that he's bad news. Basically, a real-life supervillain. A few months ago, the Builder stole Bionosoft technology. Then, he spent billions of dollars on a quantum computer. Yesterday, I discovered this."

Liz holds up a small screen. You recognize it as the device she held when she jumped into the mall fountain. A closer look reveals that the screen is divided into nine squares like a tic-tac-toe board. All nine squares are flashing a blur of letters, numbers, and shapes.

"His notes call it a Q-pad," Liz says. "It works kind of like a real-life video game checkpoint. Each time and place has its own nine-symbol combination. First, you lock in your current time and location with this button." She presses a red button, and the symbols freeze. She steps closer so you can see the combination. "Then, you return to that moment whenever you want by pressing the green button." Liz presses a second button and snaps back to where she'd been standing when she pressed the red button.

You've got so many questions. "So . . . you stole this thing? Does that mean you're a spy or something?"

"Sure, you could say that." Liz hands you the Q-pad. "Now, you're the spy."

"I don't want this!"

Liz won't take it back. "The Builder is planning something big, and this battle royale appears to be the last step. He's somewhere inside the game right now. Find him, lock in the location, then bring the Q-pad back here so I can delete him."

You're not sure what qualifies you for this superspy mission, but you're pretty sure that she has the wrong person. "Why don't you find him yourself?"

"You don't think I've tried?" Liz asks. "The Builder programmed the game to hunt me. Every time I visit Grim Island, I get killed within seconds."

"But don't you work with anyone who can help?"

A pained look flashes across Liz's face. "No."

You sigh. "Anything else I should know?"

"Yes. Stay far away from any blue cubes you find. Those are quantum cubes, and they're powering the game. If you damage them, you'll break the game and die. Like, really die. For real."

"Awesome."

"Don't worry," Liz says. "He'll have them locked up or hidden. Actually, probably both locked up *and* hidden. You shouldn't run into any."

You nod and turn, then spin back around. "Wait! What does this guy look like?"

"No idea."

"What?"

"No one has ever seen his face."

"Then how am I supposed to find him?!"

"You'll figure it out." Liz flashes a smile that's supposed to inspire confidence but instead betrays how unsure she is of this plan. "Oh! And . . ." Before Liz can finish, she glitches and disappears.

"Liz?"

You get that dizzy feeling you always experience when you reach the Endgame.

"LIZ!"

A blurry face emerges from the darkness, but it's not Liz's. It's the face from the Endgame. This time, a different section of the face is in focus. You fumble with the Q-pad to return to the last checkpoint, but none of the buttons work. The only thing on the pad is the letter *I* in the lower-right corner. Then, everything disappears.

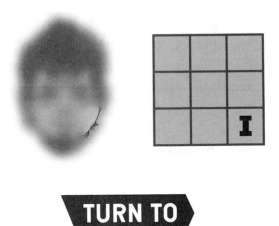

TURN TO

P.52

"HEY CHAZ, DO YOU THINK you can juggle with your eyes closed?" you ask.

Chaz whips out a blindfold. "I thought you'd never ask!"

He's so easy to trick. You crouch and creep until you reach the bush where you saw the woman. No one's there. Before you turn back, you feel a tap on your shoulder.

"AH!"

Mystery Woman puts a hand over your mouth. "We don't have much time," she says. "Come back without your team and find me . . ."

WHOMP!

A shark flies past you as if it were shot out of a cannon and swallows the woman in the brown leather jacket whole.

"NO!" you yell.

"Alpha!" Miss Eleanor shouts from Apex Airport. She's back to her normal, human form and toting a giant, shark-shaped cannon. She runs across a field to you, then wraps you in a big hug. "We missed you so!"

"Who was that lady?" you ask.

Miss Eleanor ignores your question. "Quit lollygagging and let's catch up to the team."

P. 35

X	2	M
I	3	H
B	▲	a

YOUR TEAM NEEDS WEAPONS. Mad Scientists Throughout History is an exhibit full of weapons. Seems like an easy choice. You ball your fists, flex your chest, and zap all the weapons.

Just like that, you've got access to more weapons than you can use. There's Ye Olde Froginator. Behind you is a jar of mechanical tarantulas. Miss Eleanor eyes the Power Parasol. Your team gears up just as the first enemy rounds the corner.

BANG! PEW! CROAK!

The bad guys quickly learn that they're outgunned. They retreat, but your team isn't letting them go that easily. Miss Eleanor rides her Power Parasol like a witch's broom to take out the first two enemies. Dark Pulse wraps up the third member of the team with an Electrified Lasso. Bonzai squeezes the trigger on his flamethrower, and when that doesn't work the way he wants, he chucks it at one of the fleeing foes. You finish the job with the trusty Froginator.

Easy peasy. Now, onto the Mind Meld.

TURN TO

P.28

M ❗ ACHIEVEMENT UNLOCKED
CROAK

YOU SHAKE YOUR HEAD and catch up with the rest of your team at the airport. You arrive just in time to see Bonzai hurl a pioneer man out of a helicopter by his coonskin cap. Bonzai then pounds his chest and hops into the pilot seat.

Dark Pulse takes the copilot spot, which leaves you, Chaz, and Miss Eleanor to squeeze onto the bench in the back. You give Miss Eleanor a friendly wave and lots of space to avoid another appearance by Queen of the Crocs. Chaz is not nearly as careful.

"BESTIE BOYS REUNITED!" he yells when the copter takes off. Bonzai reaches back with one of his meaty hands and tosses Chaz out of the copter. He then glares at the rest of the team which leads to a near collision with the airport terminal.

"Why don't I take over for a bit?" Dark Pulse suggests.

Bonzai rips out her steering yoke and tosses it overboard. No one takes over for Bonzai.

"Fine," Dark Pulse says through clenched teeth. "Just don't engage with anyone. There are only five squads left, and this copter is too slow."

Bonzai immediately engages with a squad of evil fairies on the ground. They all whip out Slime Sloppers when Bonzai swoops toward them.

Dark Pulse screams her frustration, then tosses you an oversized gun shaped like a lightning bolt. "Charge it."

"Uh, by charge, you mean . . ."

SPLUT!

The fairies slime both the side of the copter and Bonzai's face. He is furious.

"I MEAN CHARGE IT WITH YOUR ELECTRICITY POWER!" Dark Pulse yells.

You look at Miss Eleanor for help. "Oh dumplin', you don't know about your superpower?" Miss Eleanor asks. "You're Alpha. You've got the best power on the whole island. I wish I had yours. Mine is so unbecoming."

RATATATAT!

Great. A biplane full of Chewbacca look-alikes has joined the fight.

Dark Pulse crawls into the backseat. "If you want something done right, you have to do it yourself."

You breathe a sigh of relief. "Thank you. I just don't feel comfortable—WHOA!"

There's been a misunderstanding. Dark Pulse doesn't want to use the weapon herself. No, she wants the honor of kicking you out of the helicopter. You grab the landing skid on your way down. You're now hanging from the helicopter by one hand with two different teams shooting at you. "HELP!"

Instead of offering her hand, Dark Pulse tosses you the lightning bolt gun. "NOW, CHARGE IT!"

You fumble with the weapon. This would be much easier with two hands!

NROOOOM!

The Chewbaccas swoop in to finish the job. Only seconds left.

Mystery Woman's words come back to you: *Pay attention.*

You try to slow down. What do you see?

Certain death.

What do you hear?

The sounds of certain death.

What do you feel?

A tingle in your chest. You focus on that tingle, and sparks shoot from your hands.

ZZZZ—DING!

The weapon turns green just in time. You fire a lightning bolt at the Chewbaccas and miss badly. You fire again, but the Chewbaccas dodge. You close one eye to aim, then stop. Something on the ground catches your attention.

You look down to see Grim Island's energy plant shaking and flashing warning lights and looking for all the world like it's going to explode. Also, you're about to fly right over it.

BOOM!

The energy plant blows up before you can warn Bonzai. A water geyser shoots into the sky, destroying the Chewbaccas' plane and clipping your copter's tail.

Your copter goes down in a death spiral. Just before it crashes into a jungle, you leap. You've never leapt from a helicopter before, but you're thrilled to find that falling into a video game jungle feels just like it looks in action movies. Sure, there are a few bumps and scratches from bouncing off of trees, but you don't break every bone in your body like you would in real life. The rest of your team survives the crash too.

You all huddle behind a rock, and Miss Eleanor asks, "Where now?"

Dark Pulse slaps Bonzai's back. "Big guy. Wanna grab that health pack?"

Bonzai grunts, takes two steps beyond the rock, then—
PEW!—goes up in blue smoke.

"Snipers in the trees." Dark Pulse says. "I was afraid of that."

"Then why did you send Bonzai?!" you ask.

"There's still a health pack out there if you want it."

"NO!"

Dark Pulse slouches against the rock.

"So what do we do?" you ask.

"Nothing. They have us pinned. Another team has to take
them out."

You may not have time to wait for someone to come to
your rescue. The edge of the battle zone is catching up fast.
While you're looking at the approaching lava, something weird
happens.

Everything goes dark, and your vision suddenly zooms out—above your body, above the trees, above the volcano. Now, you're looking at a map of Grim Island. Like the map in your helmet, your teammates show up as green squares, but now, there are red circles too. Three of the circles are in the trees surrounding your rock. Suddenly, you're back.

"Whoa!" you yell. "Did anyone else see that?"

"Did you see one of them?" Dark Pulse asks.

"I saw all of them."

"Where?"

TURN TO

P. 40

Using the overhead view as a guide, locate the three trees with enemies. Working left to right, put the three numbers together. That will give you the page number for the next section. The first three words of the correct page are, "When you point."

TURN TO P. ___ ___ ___

□ △ ○

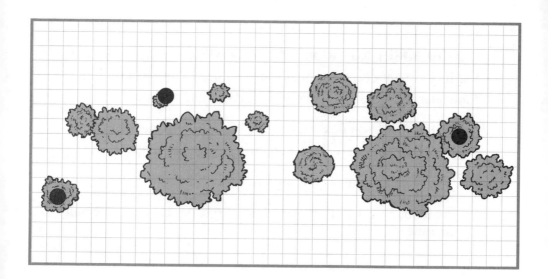

```
★ D 6
● T U
J 8 9
```

YOU MIGHT NOT HAVE ANY WEAPONS, but you feel the tingling in your chest, and that's all you need. You wait until the footsteps reach the top of the stairs before jumping out.

"AHHHH!" You flex your chest. Lightning shoots from your fingertips and fries a pair of furry critters in safari hats.

"Yes!" Chaz gives you a high five.

"Nooooo," Dark Pulse moans. "You used your special ability."

"So what?" You ask. "You're alive, aren't you?"

"Not for long."

Your team sprints toward the special exhibit, but the museum lights dim before you make it. You hear a *WUUUUUMMMM* sound coming from deep inside the museum. Someone's just activated the superweapon. Ten seconds later, your whole team gets wiped out.

0 ❗ ACHIEVEMENT UNLOCKED
NOT FOR LONG
RETURN TO CHECKPOINT ON P. 20

NO WAY. You draw the line at eating trash. You act like you didn't hear Chaz, then follow him up a mountain of garbage. When Chaz goes for a weapon, you dive underneath a crate.

"I'll hold him off while you hit him with your super shock!" Chaz yells. Then, he realizes you're missing. "Alpha?"

Do you feel bad about ditching Chaz?

"ALLLLLLLPHAAAAAA!"

Oh yeah. Real bad. But what were you going to do? You don't even know what your super shock is.

SMASH!

Gulp. Goodbye, Chaz. You huddle inside the crate waiting for the enemy to go away.

Rumble, rumble.

What was that? You thought you were alone underneath this crate.

RUMBLE, RUMBLE, RUMBLE.

The whole garbage mountain trembles. You try crawling out, but it's too late. A monstrous, slimy arm shoots out of the garbage and pulls you down into the depths of the stink.

E ❗ ACHIEVEMENT UNLOCKED
GARBAGE MONSTER
RETURN TO CHECKPOINT ON P. 23

W	■	R
J	2	M
5	◆	3

YOU KEEP TRYING to snap Chaz out of it until the ground under his feet starts crumbling. He never comes around. You finally abandon the poor guy and sprint all the way to a hill outside the dump before stopping to catch your breath. There's rustling. You jump behind a rock and look for your competition.

There! Behind that tree! It's a chicken. No, not a chicken. Someone in a way-more-realistic-than-it-needs-to-be chicken costume.

"BAWWWK!" Chicken Man screeches and whips an egg at you.

KABOOM!

The egg is a grenade!

KABOOM! KABOOM! KABOOM!

The egg grenades are coming faster now. Using pine trees and rocks as shields, you start putting distance between the chicken and yourself. Turns out, you're actually pretty good at dodging. You just might . . .

DING DING! DING DING!

Now, what's that noise? You turn to see something that's both the most surprising and least surprising sight so far: a runaway trolley headed straight for you. You try jumping, but you can't get out of the way in time. Maybe you're not that good at dodging after all.

D ❗ ACHIEVEMENT UNLOCKED
CAN'T DODGE A TROLLEY

RETURN TO CHECKPOINT ON P. 64

YOU GET THE FERRIS WHEEL CRANKING as fast as it'll go, then wave to your teammates. "Over here!"

Bonzai and Chaz start running toward you, but Bonzai is much faster thanks to his giant gallops. You look back at the control panel. It's steaming and sparking, but it hasn't blown yet. Bonzai's just a few steps away now. You've got to slow him down somehow.

"Wait!" You hold up your arms. Bonzai slams on the brakes. Wow, you can't believe that worked.

CREEEEAAK—WHOOSH!

The Ferris wheel finally spins free from its support, runs over Bonzai, and carries him across the island.

"Whoooaaa," Chaz says when he catches up to you. "Bummer about Bonzai." Then his eyes light up. "Bestie Boys to the Endgame! Can I teach you a dance?"

"First, I need you to tell me something."

"Anything!"

"What secret did Dark Pulse ask you to keep?"

Chaz's eyes get wide, then he turns and starts running. "Race you to the Endgame!"

"Wait!"

Chaz is faster than you remember. Way faster. And he's running straight toward a squad of bazooka-toting baddies. He'll choose death over spilling his secret. You've got to catch him!

To your right is a ride called The Problem. It's a trolley, just like the one you always used to see speeding across the island. Its track is unfinished and pointing straight toward Chaz. That's not a problem; it's a solution!

You hop into the trolley, and it chugs out of the station. That's when you discover the actual problem: five baby Boom-Boom bunnies tied onto the railroad tracks.

WHAT SICKO THINKS OF THESE RIDES?!

The baby Boom-Booms have all been programmed to turn their big, soulful eyes toward you and cry. Ugh! The only control in the trolley isn't a brake; it's a track switcher. Up ahead, you spot an opportunity to switch to a track with only one baby Boom-Boom.

So, to review, if you do nothing, you'll run over five baby bunnies but catch Chaz. If you switch, you only run over one bunny but set yourself on a path behind Chaz. Which do you choose?

SELECT

81 Do nothing.

82 Switch the track.

AS SOON AS YOUR SQUAD enters the ring, the bad guys round the corner.

PEW! PEW! PEW!

A force field appears around the ring and absorbs their fire. You point to the exhibit sign. "No weapons allowed. Brawlers only."

You're facing four adorable critters in safari hats. They stand no chance against your squad. But then, the fifth teammate steps up.

"BRAWWWWWL!" It's a giant who stands a full foot taller than Bonzai and appears to love brawling.

Miss Eleanor transforms into a croc and locks arms with Bonzai. The two monsters form a beefy wall, which you happily hide behind.

BOOF! WHACK! SLAM! SMOOSH!

The dynamic duo makes quick work of the four fluffy explorers. Now, only the giant is left. Bonzai picks you up. At first, you think he's saving you from an attack, but, no, he intends to use you as a bat. He swings you as hard as he can.

Is it painful? Sure. But does it work? Oh yeah. The giant topples, and your team moves on to the special exhibit.

TURN TO

P. 143

ⓘ ACHIEVEMENT UNLOCKED
BEEFY BRAWLERS

THE SUPERVILLAINS OF GRIM ISLAND sure know how to build an amusement park. Since they don't have to deal with pesky concerns like "safety" and "return customers," they can focus on one thing: fun at all costs. As a result, the roller coaster features a jump, the bumper cars have rocket boosters, and the Ferris wheel is spinning at 100 mph. You want to ride all of it.

Your team is just about to land at the roller coaster when you spot an ambush. A full squad of beady-eyed aliens is hiding inside the station. At the last second, you veer off toward the fun house. No one else on your team sees the trap.

You land on the fun house roof and hide behind an oversized balloon bunny. (It's Adventure Zone's mascot, Boom-Boom. Boom-Boom Bunny has a black eye, cast, and giant grin to illustrate the park's motto: "Dangerously Fun!") You peek out from behind Boom-Boom to see how your team handles the ambush. Then, the craziest thing happens:

There is no ambush.

The aliens could destroy your team in two seconds, but instead, they lower their weapons and stare blankly.

Your team scrambles to find you. Miss Eleanor looks at her pocket watch map and points at the fun house. They all start running. Looks like there's another squad closing in from the opposite direction too. Quick, hide!

You open a rooftop door and stumble into a security room. What good fortune! Turns out, the fun house features dozens of cameras, and you get a live feed from all of them. There's the hall of mirrors, the spinning room, and the spooky maze.

One of the security cameras picks up Chaz's voice when your team walks into the fun house. "Shouldn't we tell Alpha? Best friends don't keep secrets."

Dark Pulse grabs Chaz by his collar. "Don't you dare."

Tell Alpha what? You've got to get Chaz by himself to learn the secret.

Your team steps onto the fun house's first attraction: a swinging rope bridge suspended over a snake pit. (Dangerous! Fun!) Chaz, Bonzai, and Miss Eleanor safely cross the bridge, but Dark Pulse pauses for a moment to study her map. If you're going to get Chaz by himself, you'll need to start separating him from members of the team. Here's your first opportunity to do that. The bridge's ropes connect to the security room. Cut the correct ropes and take out the bridge.

> *Find the two ropes that connect the bridge to the ceiling.*
> *When you put those numbers together from left to right, you'll*
> *find the page number for the next section. The first sentence*
> *of the correct page is, "What did you do?!"*

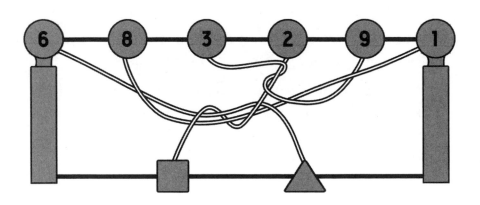

P. ___ ___

YOU SQUEEZE THE CUBE in your right hand, and it melts through your suit. You feel a cool energy course through your body. The Builder picks up a cube from the table and does the same.

Congratulations! You're now the proud owner of a quantum-powered galaxy brain. You can see a million moves ahead.

The next words out of your mouth would have surprised you just a moment ago, but they feel inevitable now. You've seen the future. Now that you've both taken a cube, there's only one way this can end. You smile at the Builder.

"Let's team up," you suggest.

R ❗ ACHIEVEMENT UNLOCKED
GALAXY BRAIN

RETURN TO CHECKPOINT ON P. 180

"ALPHA?"

You're back on the plane.

"No wayyy. Guys, check this out! It's Alpha!"

You've got to get back to Liz.

"ALPHAAAAAAA!"

You push past Chaz and strap on a parachute.

"Where are you going, good buddy?" Chaz asks. "The Bestie Boys drop together!"

You open the hatch and jump. You don't care if your teammates know where you're going. You have roughly 800 more questions, and Liz is going to answer all of them.

Actually, she's not.

When you land at the airport, you find that the symbol on the terminal is gone. The wall is solid. You feel all over, but the glitch has been fixed. Your path to Liz—the one person who can help you escape the loop—is gone.

You slump to the ground. A turkey with a musket kills you.

When you return to the plane, you slump some more. Then, you start thinking. What about that face you keep seeing? The one at the Endgame and now under the airport terminal. Could that be the Builder?

A theory starts to form. Both times you saw the face, you also saw a Q-pad symbol. Maybe the face is leading you to the Builder! You need seven more symbols to fill out the grid. Can you find the face seven more times?

"ALPHAAAAAA!" Chaz screams in your face again.

You stand straight just like you imagine a real Alpha would and make your voice as deep as you can. "At ease, soldier."

Chaz salutes you. You look around to see that your whole squad is standing at attention. Wait, was the secret to commanding your squad really just acting like a leader?!

"Where are we dropping, squad leader?" Chaz asks.

P. 54

Visit each section of the map in whatever order you'd like. Think of these sections as levels within the game. Beat the levels to find symbols for the grid on the next page. Once you find all nine symbols, turn to the page with that grid in its heading.

Museum of Villainous Excellence

Creepy Country

Chaos City

Azkaar Asylum

???

Boom-Boom's Adventure Zone

Grim Energy

SELECT

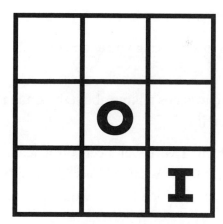

COMPLETE THE GRID. FIND ITS MATCH.
DEFEAT THE BUILDER.

AS MUCH AS THIS FACT PAINS YOU, you know it's true: You can't survive this island on your own.

You hoist Chaz over your shoulder and start running. It's not easy to outrun lava while wrangling someone who insists on dancing. You're about to give up when Chaz finally breaks his trance.

"Why aren't you dancing?" he whines.

"Because we were about to fall into lava, that's why! This whole island is crumbling!"

Chaz shakes his head. "It's just the battle zone shrinking, silly goose. Look." He taps your helmet, and a map of Grim Island takes over your view. "See this green part? That's the battle zone. It's going to keep shrinking until only one team is left."

"Then what?"

Chaz points to a smoking volcano in the middle of the island. "The Endgame."

"OK, everyone keeps talking about the Endgame, but no one will tell me what it is."

"Oh! Uh, well, I've never been on a team that got there before, so I don't know what it looks like inside. Some people say it's kind of neon, which I think would be cool, but . . ."

"I don't care what it looks like," you interrupt. "What is it?"

"Oh. Well, when only one team is left standing, the teammates go inside the volcano and fight each other to determine the ultimate winner."

"So why wouldn't you just get rid of your teammates before the Endgame?"

"Because we're besties!" Chaz looks truly offended. "Also, teams that split up almost never make it to the Endgame. You need everyone working together. Speaking of which . . ." He looks at the map on his watch. "This way!"

You check the map on your visor. It shows three green squares at Apex Airport. You don't love the idea of meeting back up with the crocodile version of Miss Eleanor, but Chaz is already strolling and whistling. Then, he stops.

"What's wrong?" you ask.

Chaz points ahead to someone dressed in a chicken suit. Chicken Man hasn't spotted you yet. "This is the perfect time to use my special ability," Chaz says. "Get ready."

"Can't we just sneak past him?"

Chaz does the opposite of sneak. He stands up and shouts, "HEY!"

Chicken Man jumps and spins, clearly expecting to get blasted in the face. Instead, Chaz takes out three balls from his back pocket and starts juggling. "LOOK!" he shouts to the chicken. "Cool, huh?" Chaz keeps the balls in the air for three whole seconds before dropping one. "Oopsie! Hang on, don't look."

Chicken Man realizes that Chaz is not dangerous, but instead a lunatic. He pulls out an egg, takes two steps toward Chaz, and . . .

ZOOOOOM!

. . . Gets flattened by a runaway trolley.

Chaz smiles. "Pretty great, huh? Everyone has a special ability, and that just happens to be mine!"

"You can smash people with rides whenever you want? That's awesome!"

"Oh no, my special ability is juggling."

You're so confused.

"It just distracts people for like a second. But it's very cool! I can do bowling pins too! Wanna see?"

"So, where did the trolley come from? And the Ferris wheel?"

Chaz shrugs. "No idea."

"THEN WHAT WAS THE POINT OF JUGGLING?!"

"The plan, as you should have figured out, was that my juggling would distract him so much that you could sneak around and . . ."

You stop listening when you glimpse something brown in a nearby bush. You squint. Are your eyes playing tricks on you? Suddenly, a head pops up. You gasp. It's the woman with the brown leather jacket that you met in the mall! She mouths two words before ducking back down.

"You. Alone."

Chaz, of course, misses the whole thing. ". . . And that's what I call the perfect plan," he finishes with a smile.

Do you ditch Chaz for the Mystery Woman?

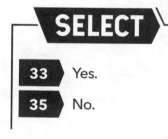

SELECT

33 Yes.

35 No.

YOU CLOSE YOUR EYES and try to picture the grid upside down. The Builder took your Q-pad, but maybe if you can remember the symbols . . .

WHOOSH!

Power surges through your body and clears your headache. Your eyes pop open. The whole world snaps into focus just like that moment the Builder's face appeared.

The kaleidoscope moves toward you. You raise your hand to protect yourself, but there's no need—it passes straight through you. Once the colorful wall is behind you, you turn and gasp. Over here, the random patterns and colors unscramble into scenes floating toward you. Each scene has its own unique Q-pad pattern. In one, you're fighting the robot pirate in the dump. In another, Chaz is dropping juggling balls in the museum. Look, there's one where a stranger is sprinting toward the creepy old cabin in the woods. After the scene flies past you, you realize that was no stranger—it was the Builder!

The Builder is revisiting your path. If he makes it all the way around the island, he'll gain the same power you have now— the power to see every possible reality. You've got to stop him before it's too late.

There's a scene where you're flying over Grim Island. You reach out to touch it.

R	U	X
6	T	9
L	P	S

You're now inside the plane by yourself. A solo mission. Excellent. Time to find the Builder.

More scenes flash in front of your face. You can see them all clearly even though they're zipping by at warp speed. There's Azkaar Asylum. Dreadful Dump. The Museum of Villainous Excellence. Oh, there's the Builder in Chaos City! You focus on that scene, and it grows larger. Suddenly, the scene swallows you whole.

★	4	L
A	I	M
Q	2	■

Wow, you've chosen your own reality! You're now inside a Chaos City apartment with a lovely renovated kitchen. You don't get much time to admire the craftsmanship before two scenes flash in front of your face: one where you get cracked in the back of the head by a television, and another where you roll forward and pick up a chair to block the blow. You choose the correct scene just in time to protect yourself. Once you complete the move, you see that you've miscalculated. The Builder's not in this apartment. Your team is. They're all scowling, even Chaz. Looks like they have a new objective.

You quickly analyze 200 possible realities.

9	●	J
◆	X	E
3	2	B

In one reality, you go after Chaz first since he's the easy one. He motions for you to come get some, but in typical Chaz fashion, that's as far as he's planned. You give him all you've got, which turns out to be way more than enough. In this scenario, you defeat Chaz but leave yourself open to the rest of your team. And, boy, are they ready to fight.

V	◆	G
H	5	8
★	C	7

In another reality, you use a power slide to slip between Bonzai's legs then flip onto the beast's back. He spins and swipes at you, which allows you to use him as a wrecking ball. Miss Eleanor and Chaz fall victim to the chaos, but Dark Pulse uses Bonzai's rage against him to lead you both into enemy fire.

N	M	X
■	P	Z
3	4	7

Maybe you should go for Dark Pulse first. Because you know her every move, you can match her speed in hand-to-hand combat. You follow one reality after another to dodge her attacks, then land a supercharged lightning punch of your own. As soon as you defeat Dark Pulse, though, Bonzai squishes you. Or Miss Eleanor chomps you. Or Chaz accidentally trips you down a stairwell. This new ability helps you fight one person easily, but it's much tougher to prepare for multiple attackers.

Oh, wait! There it is. You find one reality that leads to victory.

Find the page that contains this grid.

YOU'RE NOT READY TO COMMIT to eating the garbage chili yet, but you do pick it up and sniff it. Once you bring the can within sniffing distance of your face, the chili flashes and absorbs into your body.

YOWZA! HOT TAMALE!

The chili starts a fire in your belly. A real, honest-to-goodness fire. You open your mouth to scream for Chaz, and the fire escapes.

WHOOSH!

You vaporize a crate. Did that just happen? Did actual fire from your stomach just burn down a whole crate?! You glance at the pirate, and the look of fear on his face confirms that you do indeed wield great power. The pirate puts away his hammer and runs. You sprint after him.

WHOOSH!

You burn up a washing machine.

WHOOSH!

There goes a rusty, old van.

WHOOSH! Zing! Zoom! Pop!

You light a box of fireworks.

You aim at one of those old tube TVs, but only burp one more weak fireball. Just like that, your belly feels better. The power-up is over.

When the pirate hears that last little burp, he pulls out his hammer and points at you. You gasp. Not because of the hammer, but because of what you spot behind the pirate.

It's an out-of-control Ferris wheel.

This Ferris wheel isn't just spinning fast. No, the wheel has somehow broken free of the ride, and it's now rolling and bouncing toward the pirate.

The pirate sneers when he sees your look of fear, then gets nervous when he realizes that you're looking over his shoulder. He peeks back just in time to understand his fate.

WHOOMP!

The Ferris wheel scoops him up, then carries him over the edge of the island into lava.

You stare at the surreal scene, then look at Chaz. "Where did that come from?"

Chaz throws his arms in the air. "WE WON!"

You look around. No one else is here. "Really? We won the game?!"

"No, no, no. There are still 74 enemies between us and the Endgame. But we're the last ones left in Dreadful Dump, and that's something to celebrate! Do the Bestie Boys dance with me!" He runs to your side. "Put your hands in the air and take two steps left."

You follow Chaz's example. This delights him to no end. "PERFECT! OK, now we . . . Actually, I don't remember what comes next. No one has ever gotten this far in the Bestie Boys dance."

He stops dancing and looks up. "Oh my, how embarrassing . . ."

While Chaz stares at the sky, you're looking to the edge of the dump. It appears to be crumbling into lava. Also, the crumbling is getting closer. "Chaz?"

Chaz keeps his eyes to the sky and starts talking gibberish.

"Gnissarrabme woh ym ho . . ."

The crumbling is 10 seconds away now. "We've got to move!" you yell.

"Tfel spets owt ekat dna . . ." Chaz is now doing a backward version of the Bestie Boys dance.

"SNAP OUT OF IT!"

Five seconds left. What do you do?

SELECT

56 Save Chaz.

44 Save yourself.

YOU SPEND THE NEXT HUNDRED TRIES combing every square inch of the volcano. Although you don't find the symbol, you do discover a few interesting tidbits, like:

- The Invisible Man arrives from Chaos City and runs into the Endgame once he fights you.

- XL has a cannon on his rear end labeled "Super Stinker."

- The volcano erupts if you wait too long to enter the Endgame.

- One of the volcanic rocks looks exactly like Abraham Lincoln.

- There's a cockpit in XL's chest. And a human shadow inside the cockpit.

D ❗ ACHIEVEMENT UNLOCKED
SUPER STINKER
RETURN TO CHECKPOINT ON P. 73

YOU'D LIKE TO SAY NO, but Dark Pulse is way too intimidating to refuse. You give a half-hearted nod, prompting Dark Pulse to flash that chicken-eating grin again and rip all five backpacks off the wall. She opens a hatch and tosses three of them out the opening.

"Those are our parachutes!" Chaz yells.

Dark Pulse straps on one of the remaining chutes and tosses you the other. Then, she grabs your arm and jumps out of the plane.

You fumble with your parachute all the way to the ground. Then, an instant before you pancake on the go-kart track, the chute deploys. You're safe—for about two seconds.

Another squad closes in on you and Dark Pulse. A mad scientist, a grandmother, and a tiny man dressed in old-timey military garb all rush in for an easy kill.

"Super shock. Now!" Dark Pulse instructs.

"Super what?"

The tiny general picks up something that looks like a weaponized hair dryer.

"Your special ability! Do it!"

"I don't know what that is!"

"I WANT A NEW TEAM!" Dark Pulse screams before getting fried by the hair dryer.

E ❗ ACHIEVEMENT UNLOCKED
NEW TEAM
RETURN TO CHECKPOINT ON P. 15

YOU SNEAK BEHIND MISS ELEANOR and steal her pocket watch. Then, you climb back to the trapdoor. You make it all the way to the top rung of the ladder undetected before—*CLANG!*—your foot slips.

"Alpha!" Chaz yells.

The team stumbles over themselves to reach you. Fortunately, you have a head start. You scramble through the security room, stumble onto the roof, push past Boom-Boom, then jump toward the bumper cars.

"GRRR!" Miss Eleanor growls when she emerges from the fun house as a croc.

You toss her watch into a bumper car and stick out your tongue to make sure she's crazy with rage. It works.

Miss Eleanor snaps and slobbers all the way to the rocket-powered bumper cars. The ride powers on as soon as she reaches it.

SLAM!

She doesn't stand a chance. Now, there's just one teammate standing between you and Chaz, and you know just the ride to take care of him.

Boom-Boom's Adventure Zone has a strange security system for its Ferris wheel. Turn the page to find the ride's control panel. The right and left side of the panel both have Boom-Boom bunnies dressed in different costumes. To unleash the Ferris wheel, find the one pair of bunnies that match perfectly. The first five words of the correct page read, "You get the Ferris wheel."

TURN TO P. _____ _____

□ △

```
Z 7 ★
● F 3
4 M w
```

YOU MIGHT NOT HAVE any weapons or places to run, but you do have something even more valuable: an expendable member of your team.

"Start juggling," you tell Chaz.

"I THOUGHT YOU'D NEVER ASK!" He pulls out three balls and puts on a little show, complete with humming and hip wiggles.

Dark Pulse gives you a weird look, which you return with a wink. You've seen this performance enough times to know that Chaz will eventually mess up. And when he does . . .

"Oopsie!" Chaz says right on cue. His ball rolls into the hallway, and he chases after it.

PEW! PEW! PEW!

"Go, go, go!" you yell to your team.

You escape with Bonzai, Miss Eleanor, and Dark Pulse while the enemy squad fires at Chaz. Your team rounds a corner to find a row of villainous exhibits. Pick one to engage the enemy on your terms. There's a wrestling ring to honor bare-knuckle brawlers. That would be perfect for Bonzai. Then, there's the prehistoric monsters exhibit with a jungle setting where Dark Pulse could wreak havoc. Finally, there's a mad scientist section with tons of old weapons just waiting to be recharged.

SELECT

48 Wrestling ring.

22 Prehistoric monsters.

34 Mad scientist.

YOU GAVE YOURSELF too much credit for reaching the Endgame on your first try. Turns out, it's almost impossible to die before the Endgame if you follow two simple rules:

1. Stick with your crew. Fortunately, they make this simple by following you like nervous puppies all the time. As long as they're with you, you're safe. If you manage to shake them, even for a few seconds, another enemy always seems to find you.

2. Put up a fight. You don't have to win every battle. Actually, you don't have to win any battles. But you have to at least pretend like you care about the game. Once you start passing up weapons, you're dead.

If you follow those two rules, you're on rails to the Endgame. If you don't, then it's a quick death and return to the beginning. You're a prisoner, doomed to repeat the same sequence over and over and over.

The one thing that never repeats, no matter what you do, is the woman in the brown leather jacket. Eventually, you give up your search and go with the flow.

Hours pass. Maybe days. There's no way to know. You're so familiar with the loop by now that you could sleepwalk through it.

Dump. Airport. Helicopter. Jungle. Endgame. Repeat.

Dump. Airport. Helicopter. Jungle. Endgame. Repeat.

Dump. Air . . .

Wait.

On your 389th trip to the airport, you spot something. Maybe it's always been there, maybe it just appeared. It's a little blue symbol on the side of the terminal that looks just like a thousand other corporate logos. Except you've seen this one somewhere else. But where?

SELECT

161 Dump.

67 Endgame.

85 Mall.

"ALPHA?"

You open your eyes. It's Chaz. You're back on the plane.

"No wayyy. Guys, check this out! It's Alpha!"

You rub your head. What's going on?

"Chaz, be cool."

"WE HAVE ALPHAAAAAA!"

"Stop." You leap to your feet. "We already did this."

Chaz shakes his head. "First time for me, partner! Welcome to the Bestie Boys!"

Bonzai growls. You step between the two of them. "Don't fight! Please. Someone just tell me what happened in the Endgame."

"You don't know about the Endgame?" Dark Pulse asks.

You turn around. "Yes! I was there! With you! Don't you remember?"

Dark Pulse lays a paw on your shoulder. "Suuure, I remember," she replies in a tone that says she definitely doesn't remember. "Hey, why don't we return there? Just you and me?"

You back up. "Don't do this."

"What are y'all darlings discussin'?" Miss Eleanor asks.

BOOM! BOOF!

Bonzai's upset over Chaz's "Bestie Boys" comment again. You'd better start talking faster if you want to stop this next part. "The Endgame. All three of us were there. Plus, the creepy face. Did either of you see that creepy face?"

Both Dark Pulse and Miss Eleanor stare at you blankly, then Dark Pulse says, "Alpha wanted to ditch you. Called you a loser."

"DON'T DO THIS AGAIN!"

Miss Eleanor transforms into the crocodile, then tosses both you and Chaz out of the plane. You land at the dump. "Don't shoot that," you warn Chaz when he picks up the diaper arrow. He shoots it anyway, and the pirate chases you.

"EAT THE CHILI!" Chaz shouts. You sigh. Might as well play this out like last time until you can talk to the woman in the brown leather jacket.

Except she never shows.

You search the exact bush where you'd seen her last time. No one's back there. "Excuse me," you ask Miss Eleanor when you board the helicopter. "Have you seen someone wearing a brown leather jacket?"

"Well, fiddledeedee, I don't recall that I have." Her eyes narrow. "Have you?"

"No."

"Good. The last thing we need around these parts is another dark-hearted varmint in a leather jacket."

The real dark-hearted varmint, of course, is the fox sitting in the copilot seat. Like last time, Dark Pulse betrays your team over and over until you reach the Endgame. You keep a close eye on her. Does she know more than she's letting on?

When you reach the Endgame this time, you know what to expect. You fight to keep focus as darkness closes in and get rewarded by a glimpse of some sort of arena. Then, there's the grid. You see that it's not just a circle in the middle of a square; it's a circle in the middle of a tic-tac-toe grid. Then, there's the creepy face. You can see it clearer now. You hold on as long as you can before—

"Alpha?"

You're back in the plane with Chaz.

You live the same loop again . . .

And again . . .

And again.

Each time, it's the same thing. No matter what you say, Bonzai always fights Chaz on the plane. No matter how hard you struggle, you always get thrown out at the dump. And no matter where you look, you can't find the Mystery Woman.

How do you break the cycle?

SELECT

98 Convince your team this is a video game.

79 Explore on your own.

19 Find a cheat code.

73 Give up.

"ALPHA!" Miss Eleanor cheers when you cross her flashlight. "I'm so glad we found you!"

Bonzai grabs your arm a little too hard and grunts. Chaz gives you a big hug. "Never leave again!"

Bonzai leads you through the maze into a spinning room. When Chaz walks into the room, he presses a button that spins the room so fast that the whole team gets thrown against the wall.

"GRRR!" Bonzai growls.

From there, you enter the hall of mirrors, and Chaz can't help himself in here either. He fiddles with a dial, which causes a laser beam to bounce off every mirror in the hall.

"Wasn't me!" Chaz exclaims.

Chaz resists the urge to touch more stuff until he reaches the exit. Next to the door is a big lever. Chaz must pull it.

CHOMP!

Bear traps fall from the ceiling and land on your team. What a fun addition to this house.

A ❗ ACHIEVEMENT UNLOCKED
"FUN" HOUSE

RETURN TO CHECKPOINT ON P. 26

YOUR TEAMMATES ARE WAY CLINGIER than you noticed at first. They may not always act like they want you around, but every time you try venturing out on your own, they turn into world-class clingers.

You brainstorm creative ways to escape your team. What happens if you push them all out of the plane? Bonzai drags you along for the ride. What about finding someone on another squad to eliminate your team? No one will do the honors. Maybe if you ask politely to spend some time away from your team? Chaz cries, Bonzai bashes you on the head, Miss Eleanor bites your leg, and Dark Pulse repeatedly calls you a creep.

On the rare occasion that you do get away, an enemy kills you almost immediately. Even in places where you're sure there wasn't an enemy, one always shows up the second your team isn't around. The game must want you to stick with your team. But why?

G ❗ ACHIEVEMENT UNLOCKED
WORLD-CLASS CLINGERS

RETURN TO CHECKPOINT ON P. 75

GRIM ISLAND has a lot going against it. It's surrounded by lava, for example. Not great. Also, it's home to nearly as many deadly creatures as Australia. But one area where the island shines is its robust farmers market. Next time you're here, you'll have to sample the peaches. They look delightful.

For now, though, you're busy dodging incoming fire. You run up a wall (which doesn't feel like something you could have done earlier) and start bouncing off of awnings like you're at a trampoline park. All of your jumping and spinning attracts fire from three different teams, revealing their positions to Bonzai and Miss Eleanor.

Miss Eleanor clenches her fists to change into the crocodile, then absolutely cleans up alongside Bonzai. The two monsters snort and claw and pound their chests as they take down three whole teams. They are having a great time.

Maybe too great.

Miss Eleanor gets a little too excited after one kill and makes the classic Chaz mistake of choreographing a dance in the middle of battle. She pays for it.

Now, it's just you and Bonzai versus the team of snipers at the top of the glass tower. Bonzai grunts, then climbs the skyscraper like King Kong. Do you join him or take the stairs inside?

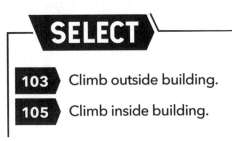

SELECT

103 Climb outside building.

105 Climb inside building.

CHAZ IS THE MOST IMPORTANT thing here, not some fake video game bunnies. You decide to keep the course, even though you feel terrible about running over the baby Boom-Booms.

Then, something happens that makes you feel even more terrible. Chaz starts running backward. Noooo, you forgot that this always happens after the Ferris wheel. Now, you're going to lose both Chaz and the baby bunnies!

Suddenly, you have an idea. It's not going to help you reach Chaz, but it feels like the right thing to do.

"HEY!" you scream at the bazooka-toting squad that Chaz had been running toward. "Bet you can't hit me!"

BOOM!

They do, in fact, hit you. Or at least your trolley. You dive from the vehicle just before their rocket hits it, and the trolley blows up just before it runs over the bunnies. Everyone wins.

Except for Chaz. He runs backward out of the battle zone and into the lava.

❶ ACHIEVEMENT UNLOCKED
THE TROLLEY PROBLEM

RETURN TO CHECKPOINT ON P. 45

A THEORY HAS BEEN BREWING in the back of your head for a while now, and this seems like the perfect time to test it. You've noticed that certain things always happen at certain times in this game. First, the runaway Ferris wheel that happens four minutes into a game. Now that you've broken it free, it's currently bouncing across the island. Two minutes after that, there's a runaway trolley. Thanks to you, that's on its way too.

But there's one event that always happens between the Ferris wheel and the trolley. And that event—not the fake bunnies—makes you switch tracks.

SHING!

As soon as you switch tracks, two things happen:

1. A ramp appears, allowing the trolley to jump the baby Boom-Boom.

2. Chaz starts running backward, right on schedule.

You were right! You're still not sure how everything's connected, but this confirms that big events happen in the same exact way at the same exact time whenever you land on the island.

You pull Chaz into the trolley just before it runs him over. When he finally stops his backward babbling, you grill him. "What do you need to tell me?"

Chaz's face lights up. "Knock, knock."

"No jokes! What do you need to tell me?"

Chaz holds up a finger like he's going to talk, then tries jumping out of the trolley. You grab his shirt before he hits the ground. Maybe you can try a gentler approach. "OK, I won't ask about that. I just want to get to know you better. Where do you live?"

Chaz looks relieved that he can finally drop his guard. "I still live at home, but that's only because I don't get benefits with my current henchman job. I'm hoping to get into the union so I can get health insurance and move into my own place."

This is not the answer you were expecting. "Um, there's no such thing as a henchmen's union."

Chaz blinks in confusion. "How do you think we get benefits? Do you think supervillains would actually pay for health insurance on their own? They're supervillains!"

Something about this answer triggers a realization. "You're not a regular video game character," you say slowly.

"I'm a henchman." Chaz replies proudly.

"Right! That's what I mean. Because if you were a regular video game character, you couldn't have a conversation with me. You'd just say whatever you were programmed to say."

"I'm not programmed to say anything."

"But you're also not a real person like me."

Chaz stops contributing to the conversation and lets you figure it out on your own.

"Because if you were a real person, you wouldn't be talking about henchmen unions. You'd be trying to solve this."

Chaz smiles.

"Sooo . . ." You look into Chaz's eyes. "I don't know who you are." You get that woozy feeling again.

"If you don't know who I am," Chaz says with a knowing grin, "then maybe you . . ."

That's as far as he gets before you're plunged back into darkness. The last thing you see is Chaz's face morph into the creepy face. Then, you spot the grid.

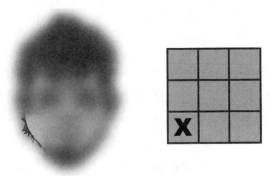

TURN TO

P. 54

THAT'S THE BLUE SYMBOL at the bottom of the mall fountain! Mystery Woman jumped straight into that symbol right after she told you to pay attention. You've got to do the same, but you can't let your teammates see you.

Your squad has already loaded into the helicopter, and Bonzai is ready to leave.

"Alpha!" Dark Pulse yells. "Let's go!"

You climb into the backseat, and Bonzai lifts off. "Sorry I'm late. I was just . . ." Your voice trails off when you see Chaz rubbing his hands together. Of course! This is the perfect opportunity to escape the watchful eyes of your teammates. You scooch past Miss Eleanor and put your arm around Chaz just in time for his favorite line.

"BESTIE BOYS REUNITED!" you both yell in unison.

Bonzai grabs both of you in a fit of rage and throws you out of the helicopter.

Chaz puts his hands behind his head and closes his eyes just like he does every time he gets thrown out of an aircraft. Perfect. Now, no one will see you. You angle your body toward the terminal and zoom straight toward the symbol, just like Mystery Woman did at the mall.

At the last second, you lose your nerve. You're going too fast! You squeeze your eyes closed and prepare for a terrible headache.

WHOOSH!

You pass right through the wall. Then, you tumble through darkness for a while before landing on your feet.

Where are you? Wherever it is happens to be pitch black. After a few seconds of darkness, lights on your suit flicker to reveal that you're underneath the airport. There are polygon shapes everywhere, but this definitely isn't an official area of the game.

You try exploring, but there aren't many places to look. Just four walls, some shapes on a ceiling, and a staircase.

Wait a second. Someone painted red lines on each of the stairs. Is this some kind of puzzle? Maybe a code? You study the lines for a long time. So long that you eventually need to rest.

When you lie on the ground, you gasp. From this angle, you can finally read the message!

TURN TO

P. 29

THE ARCHITECT OF CHAOS CITY appears to have been an easily distracted two-year-old. Hundreds of cube apartments form giant mounds instead of straight towers. Streets twist and knot and dead-end for no reason. The modern glass skyscraper in the middle of the city gives you an actual headache when you look at it.

The supervillains, on the other hand, embrace it all. Dozens of villains join your squad in descending onto the city. This is by far the most popular destination on all of Grim Island. When teams land, they scurry into apartments and reemerge with light saber spears and blades that sprout their own blades and ray guns that look too big to carry.

Dark Pulse leads your squad toward a roof where a troll has just picked up a bazooka-sized bowling pin. The troll aims, and Dark Pulse narrows her eyes. She's daring him to fire.

SHOONK!

He fires. Dark Pulse easily dodges the bowling ball rocket, and now the troll's in trouble. (The Bazooka Bowler, you see, is notoriously difficult to reload.) The troll fumbles with the weapon, but Bonzai kicks him off the roof before he can fire another shot.

Your team enters the apartment through the roof just as a penguin dressed in an actual tuxedo crashes through the door. Miss Eleanor wallops the penguin with a frying pan.

BOOM!

A unicorn carrying a concerning amount of explosives blows a hole in the wall. She tosses a grenade at your team, but Dark Pulse bats it back with a lamp.

BOOM again!

Everyone picks up a weapon and heads downs to the next floor. "Alpha! Cactus!" Chaz points to something in the corner that looks like a deflated cactus. It's glowing, though, so maybe it's a weapon?

As soon as you touch the cactus, it wraps itself around your body and inflates. Now, you look like the mascot of a tacky taco restaurant.

"Wait up!" You waddle toward your team but only get three steps before a cat that looks suspiciously like Garfield crashes onto your head.

"EEEEEEE!" The cat scoots around the room in a panic. It's got 100 cactus needles sticking out of its butt. You watch in shock as it disappears in a puff of blue smoke.

DING!

You've earned your first elimination in the city.

You sprint downstairs to share the great news with your teammates. Before you can reach them, a buck wearing an orange hunting vest and camouflage hat that says, "FEAR THE DEER!" blocks your path. Still high off of your Garfield takedown, you slap the deer's back.

"WELCOME TO THE PARTY, PAL!"

You've never uttered the phrase "welcome to the party" before in your whole life—not even at a real party. And you've certainly never called anyone "pal." But you've never felt this confident before either. Your cactus has the same effect on the deer as it did on Garfield. Now, you have two kills.

You catch up to your crew just in time to see Chaz get clobbered by a black swan. You dive onto the swan for your third kill of the match.

"I AM INVINCIBLE!" you scream just as your suit disappears.

Dark Pulse tosses you a brown pebble. You don't have time to ask if this is a souvenir or something you might actually need because she's already climbing out of the fire escape. She looks up to the roof, then down at the alley. She starts climbing toward the roof. Bonzai jumps into the alley. Where do you go?

SELECT

| 99 | Follow Dark Pulse. |
| 96 | Follow Bonzai. |

MISS ELEANOR AND BONZAI opt for the farmers market, while you veer toward the fitness facility alone. You don't need backup. You're Alpha.

Instead of the play-by-play, here's a list of all the enemies you eliminate:

- A ninja who thought he was being sneaky with a blowgun and snorkel in the lap pool

- A six-foot slice of New York–style pizza outfitted in full army fatigues

- Three corgis dressed as ghosts who were not fooling *anyone*

- A T. rex just trying to squeeze in some bicep curls

- Mr. and Mrs. Snowman who meet an untimely demise inside a sauna

- A janitor yelling "Don't worry! I'm just a janitor!"

After clearing the gym, you run outside in time to see Miss Eleanor go down. It's just you and Bonzai versus the snipers now. Bonzai takes one look at you, snorts, then begins climbing the glass skyscraper like King Kong. Do you join him or take the stairs?

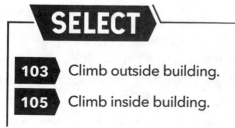

SELECT

103 Climb outside building.

105 Climb inside building.

WAY BACK AT THE BEGINNING of your journey, you noticed something strange while flying over the lava sea. You've never mentioned the spot to anyone, although you do check on it from time to time.

A patch of lava the size of a doghouse doesn't behave like the surrounding sea. While the rest of the lava ripples like ocean water, this patch remains frozen in place. That's it. Nothing crazy. It's probably a meaningless glitch. But then again, maybe it's not. Time to check it out.

"Let's drop at that outpost!" You point to a fort at the edge of the island. Dark Pulse makes a face but jumps anyway. Everyone else follows her lead, with you taking up the rear. You deploy your parachute right away and angle toward the lava sea.

"Buddy! Wait!" Chaz shouts when he notices you've separated from the group. He's too late to do anything about it. You keep gliding until you're low enough to feel the heat from the lava, but the glitch still looks like it's a mile away.

Somehow, you manage to reach the spot. You pass right through it just like the false wall at the airport terminal. You fall through darkness for a few seconds before landing on your feet.

Unlike the airport terminal, this secret area looks like it gets heavy use. It's a weird room for someone to spend a lot of time in—the place is a hodgepodge of different styles. To your left, for example, is a giant blueprint hanging on the wall. Under the blueprint is an antique desk and a fancy chessboard. Everything on this side of the room looks like it belongs in an old, rich person's study. But the right side of the room looks like something out of Star Wars. On that side, there's smoke, neon, and holograms. You reach out to touch one of the holograms, then jump back when it fritzes, pops, then disappears.

When you turn around, your heart starts pumping faster. There's a door. Light glows underneath. You slowly step toward the door and reach for the handle.

Locked.

Surely there's a key around somewhere.

THUNK!

Whoa! You jump and spin to find that Miss Eleanor has landed. "Whew!" she wipes her brow. "Honeybun, you can't go soarin' off by your little lonesome!"

"Oh! I, uh . . ." Your voice trails off when you see that the wall behind Miss Eleanor has transformed into a black-and-white saloon from an old Western. The blueprint has changed into wanted posters.

"Can I help you with something, sugar?" Miss Eleanor says in a tone that feels a little like a threat.

You take a step back and survey the ever-changing room. You've got to find that key.

On the next page, search each panel of the grid for the key.
Once you find it, turn to that panel's page number to reach the next
area. Before you pick up the key, though, you may want to explore some
of the other panels by turning to their page numbers. You just might
learn something interesting.

YOU'LL TAKE YOUR CHANCES with Bonzai. When you jump down, Dark Pulse pokes her head over the roof. "I need you to . . ."

POW!

Just like that, she explodes.

Usually, this is the point where you'd start to panic. Usually, you'd look for a hiding spot. Not this time. This time, you're an action hero. You're Alpha.

You hop onto a nearby motorcycle and rev the engine. Bonzai takes that as his signal to start rampaging through the streets. The two of you make quite a team. Bonzai leads the charge, flattening anyone who stands up to him. You clean up enemies who got out of the way. At one point, you use an overturned hot dog stand as a ramp, which feels like a pretty advanced move for someone who's never ridden a motorcycle before. After you clear the streets, you meet Miss Eleanor behind a convenience store.

Ping! Ping!

Snipers! You can take them out by getting to the skyscraper. There are two paths to the tower: one through the farmers market and the other through a fitness center. Which path do you take?

SELECT

80 Farmers market.

91 Fitness center.

MAYBE THERE'S ANOTHER WAY to open the door. You edge closer to it.

"How about moseying over here to keep me company?" Miss Eleanor asks. "I'm feelin' mighty lonesome."

You nod but keep shuffling toward the door. "Will do! Yes. For sure."

Miss Eleanor narrows her eyes when she sees where you're headed. "I need you."

Keep going. Just a few more feet. "Totally! Same."

Miss Eleanor's tone shifts dramatically. "Don't touch that door!"

You leap for the door, and Miss Eleanor leaps toward you. She transforms into the crocodile.

Perfect. You wait until the last second, then spin out of the way. You're playing matador here, hoping Miss Eleanor's bull rush will crash down the door.

That does not happen. Pretty much the opposite happens. Instead of knocking down the door, Miss Eleanor gets a mouthful of doorknob. She spits it out, rubs her snout, then cracks a toothy grin. You're trapped with her now.

❗ ACHIEVEMENT UNLOCKED

BULL IN A BOX

RETURN TO CHECKPOINT ON P. 94

"FOR THE TENTH TIME, this is a video game!"

You're lying. This isn't the tenth time you've had this conversation on the plane. It's at least the hundredth.

"If we were in a video game, could I do this?" Chaz asks as he pulls out his juggling balls.

"Punch him," you tell Bonzai. Bonzai is happy to oblige. "Now, did that hurt?" you ask Chaz.

"Obviously not. We're on the same team."

"Exactly! That's not a thing in real life! Only video games!"

Miss Eleanor has an "agree to disagree" look on her face, so you step on her toe. "Mercy!" she squeals. You step on it again. That brings out Miss Croc.

"Does anyone think she could do that if this weren't a video game?"

"She's a supervillain," Dark Pulse says like you're the biggest dummy in the world.

"SUPERVILLAINS AREN'T REAL!"

This particular supervillain bites your arm and throws you out of the plane. Time to try again.

RETURN TO CHECKPOINT ON P. 75

YOU CLIMB ONTO THE ROOF with Dark Pulse. Miss Eleanor joins you too. Dark Pulse motions for you to come close while she hops from roof to roof. "I need you to . . ."

BOOM!

Dark Pulse explodes.

"Heeheehee!" A squad of small, squeaky critters down below are giggling and dancing like they've just won the game. Rage boils inside you. Why? It's not like Dark Pulse was your best friend. She was likely only seconds away from betraying you. Doesn't matter. You *must* avenge your teammate. So you use the only weapon you have: the pebble. Fortunately, this isn't just any pebble. It's a magic boulder.

BUMP! BUMP! CRASH!

Once you throw the pebble, it grows to the size of a boulder and tears down the mound of apartments. By the time those terrible critters realize what's about to happen, they get crunched. You sprint to the boulder, pick it up like it weighs nothing, then hurl it at another team. You crunch them too. You hop to the ground where you're joined by Miss Eleanor and Bonzai.

Ping! Ping! Ping!

Snipers on top of the skyscraper start firing at your squad. You've got to reach the tower. Looks like you can travel through the farmers market or the fitness center. Which do you choose?

SELECT

80 Farmers market.

91 Fitness center.

Check out the wanted posters below to learn more about your team.

WANTED
ALPHA
REWARD: $1,000,000
Electrified and extremely dangerous.

WANTED
DARK PULSE
REWARD: $50,000
Double-crossin' no-good varmint.

WANTED
BONZAI
REWARD: $10,000
Dumb brute. Easy to lure into traps.

WANTED
MISS ELEANOR
REWARD: $10,000
Proper belle above all else. Until angered.

WANTED
CHAZ
REWARD: $0
Harmless clown. Do not befriend.

⚠ ACHIEVEMENT UNLOCKED
NO-GOOD VARMINTS
RETURN TO CHECKPOINT ON P. 94

MISS ELEANOR JOINS YOU on your cemetery excursion. This is your first time visiting a cemetery at night because you're not a werewolf or a weirdo, and (big surprise) it's creepier than you'd imagined. You try calming yourself by reading some of the tombstones. There's Baron von Boom. Born January 22, 1888, died . . . It says today's date. Hmm, weird. You go to the next one. Lonnie Llama. Born May 11, 2002, died . . .

"Why do all of these tombstones show today's date?" you ask Miss Eleanor.

"Well, sweetie . . ."

ZING!

You've got company. A plasma blast lights up the graveyard as it flies past your head. You and Miss Eleanor start running.

SHUNK!

Another blast hits the ground on your left. You're in the open now. You sneak a peek over your shoulder and find a vampire aiming straight at you. You're dead.

SHUNK!

Then, suddenly, you're saved. A new tombstone pops up behind you just in time to block the shot. You huddle with Miss Eleanor behind the monument. "Every time someone dies on Grim Island, their tombstone appears in Sinners' Cemetery," Miss Eleanor explains. She pats the inscription. "Thank you, kindly, Ballistics Bill."

Crunch. Crunch. Crunch.

The vampire's footsteps are approaching. Miss Eleanor waits until he's almost on top of you before clenching her fists. "ARRRRGH!" She starts chasing the vampire.

Here's your chance to explore the graveyard. Tombstones that appear for every death in the game is actually a pretty cool idea. You walk up a hill to get a better view of the monuments as they appear. When you reach the top of the hill, your jaw drops. This isn't the whole graveyard. Not even close. On the other side of the hill are more tombstones than you could possibly count. The name on the first one? Alpha.

❗ ACHIEVEMENT UNLOCKED
RIP ALPHA
RETURN TO CHECKPOINT ON P. 141

YOU COULD TAKE ON the world right now. Climbing a little skyscraper is nothing. You punch glass and scramble up the tower with Bonzai. Even though you're under attack from all angles, you always have the perfect dodge ready. It feels like you're climbing by muscle memory even though this is your first trip up the tower. This *is* your first trip, right?

"Watch your left!" you yell to Bonzai.

"UH?!" he grunts.

Bonzai is correct to grunt in confusion. Nothing's over there. But three seconds later, a rocket whistles by Bonzai's left side.

"Hang on!" you yell just before an explosion rumbles inside the building. The tower creaks, then leans, then topples over. Your instincts tell you how long to hold on before leaping to safety. Bonzai's not so lucky.

When you reach the ground, you survey the damage and find that you're the last one standing in Chaos City. Onto the Endgame.

P.110

THE CONTENTS OF THIS TABLE have changed three times since you've been in this room. First, there were sketches. Next, you noticed cardboard cutouts. Now, it's full of miniature prototypes. They're actually pretty cute. When you pick them up, your helmet displays information about each prototype.

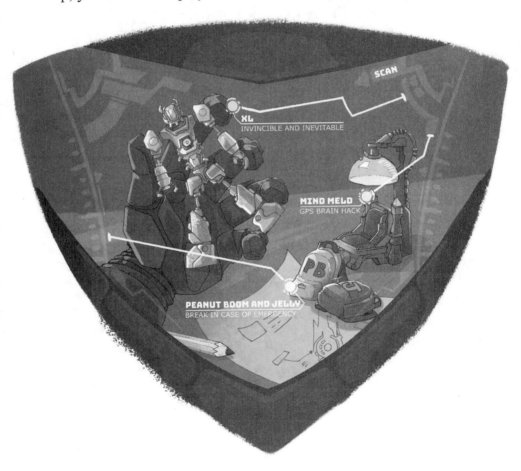

SCAN

XL
INVINCIBLE AND INEVITABLE

MIND MELD
GPS BRAIN HACK

PEANUT BOOM AND JELLY
BREAK IN CASE OF EMERGENCY

N

⊘ ACHIEVEMENT UNLOCKED
COLLECTIBLES

RETURN TO CHECKPOINT ON P. 94

INSIDE THE BUILDING, you find a glass elevator and spiral staircase. The elevator is rigged to explode when someone touches it. You can't explain how you know; you just know.

You sprint up exactly 53 stairs, then perform a front flip. When you land, you notice that you've just cleared three laser trip wire. Wait, how did you know about those too? Your instincts lead you to dance up the stairs, expertly dodging mines and spike traps. Then, when you've almost reached the top—

BOOM!

A fireball runs up the elevator shaft. Someone set off the trap, even though you're the only one in the building. The explosion triggers a series of other explosions up the staircase, causing the skyscraper to lean.

You sprint to the roof just in time to see the snipers fall off the tower. You hold on to a railing, then flip yourself into the air at precisely the right moment to survive the fall.

When you reach the ground, you survey the damage. Doesn't look like Bonzai made it. You're the last survivor of Chaos City. Onto the Endgame.

TURN TO

P. 110

YOU RUN TO A FARM, grab two pairs of exploding nunchucks, then climb a water tower. XL powers up his attack, while you charge your electricity. Then, just before he unleashes a flurry of missiles, you channel a blast through the water tower.

PSSSSHHHHH!

The tower shoots a jet of water, propelling you over the missiles and onto XL's shoulder. You stuff one pair of nunchucks into the left shoulder joint, then jump, kick, and flip as the robot swipes at you. At the height of your jump, you throw the second pair of nunchucks into XL's right shoulder joint, then bounce off his head and land on a barn roof.

BOOM! BOOM!

The nunchucks blow the arms clean off of XL. Excellent. One more step to your plan. You slide down the roof and swipe an Everliving Tar Blaster. Then, you take off toward the jungle. XL rumbles after you, but without his arms, he can't use any of his long-range weapons. You grab one more Everliving Tar Blaster. You are now armed to the gills with tar.

You sprint to the edge of the battle zone. The island is crumbling into lava just a few feet ahead. This is where you make your stand. You turn to face the giant mech.

XL can't smile because he doesn't have lips, but, oh, he wants to smile so much. He has you. You stand your ground while the earth crumbles behind you and the armless robot charges in front of you. Then, a split second before XL squishes you, you unleash everliving tar. After emptying both of your tar blasters onto the ground, you dive away.

It works. XL gets stuck. He twists and squirms but can't free himself before falling into lava. Now, it's just you and the Builder. You don't have to look at the possibilities to know where to find him. He's collecting the final symbol at the Endgame.

When you step inside the volcano this time, there's no darkness. No dizziness. No shadows. You stoop to pick up the Q-pad that the Builder left at the Endgame entrance. He's done it, hasn't he? The Builder doesn't need this anymore. He can choose his own reality now.

The Builder smiles and cracks his knuckles when he sees you. This is going to be your toughest battle yet.

Karate. Jujitsu. Kung fu. Something called "rough and tumble," which is mostly just eye gouging. You try every style of mixed martial arts ever devised, but the Builder is ready for all of it.

You try escaping the Builder. Not possible. Now that the Builder can see every possible reality, he's able to follow you across time and space.

There's one reality where all you do is talk. The Builder tells you all his evil plans. About how he was *this close* to releasing a berry into the world that would turn everyone into monsters. About how the first thing he's going to do with his new power is take over Hawaii so he can set up a real supervillain base in a real volcano. About how he is the greatest supervillain of all time. He talks and talks and talks but never actually does anything because he knows you'll be there to stop him.

You circle each other like lions. To an observer, this looks like the least interesting fight of all time. But inside both of your heads are a million battles happening at once. Every single fight ends in a draw. You can see all of his moves, and he can see all of yours. You can't beat the Builder at this game. To borrow a chess term, you're locked in a stalemate.

Suddenly, you remember the blue cubes.

Liz warned you about quantum cubes that held the power to destroy both you and the game. What if you found those? You scroll through all sorts of realities but can't land on one that takes you to the cubes. Liz said the Builder would lock them up or hide them. Maybe both.

Wait. You know a spot that fits that description. You try to picture it, but the reality won't come. You pull out the Q-pad and search the history.

"What's the matter?" the Builder sneers. "Can't do it in your head anymore?"

There it is—the locked door inside the blueprint room. Didn't it seem like something else should have been in there? What if that's the hiding spot? You stare at the Q-pad grid and try a new trick you've learned: turning it upside down.

Turn to the grid at the bottom of page 130, flip the book around, then find the page with that new grid. Redrawing this new version of the grid on a separate piece of paper might make your search easier.

P. 130 AND ROTATE BOOK

YOU SPRINT THROUGH TOWN, collecting every weapon you can before the lava comes. Part of you feels like you don't even need the weapons. You're Alpha after all. You're the best fighter on the planet.

After you leave the city, the Grim Island map flashes in your helmet, displaying the location of every enemy. Could this be any easier? Five enemies left. Four enemies left. Three. Two. One.

The Endgame is open.

This feels like the greatest moment of your life. You're so wrapped up in the thrill of the game that you can't even remember any of your previous tries, let alone life before the game. Right now, you *are* Alpha.

Wait a second. What is that? Up ahead.

It's a shadow. Not like a villain dressed in black who might call himself "The Shadow," but actual, human-shaped darkness. It's running toward the Endgame.

You're filled with rage. Nothing comes between you and your achievement. You fire every weapon you have. They all pass through the shadow. You scream a war cry. It doesn't hear you.

You charge then launch yourself at its chest. It's like tackling water. You knock down the shadow but land on the other side empty-handed. It stands up, then you tackle it again.

The battle moves to the ground with you elbowing and punching and trying to pin the shadow. Not once does it occur to you that this exact scenario has played out dozens of times before, except you've always been on the other side.

Then, you hear the sound of metal screeching against metal. A shadow falls across your battle. You look up to see XL the 100-foot-tall robot clomping toward the Endgame. Another challenger? *Nothing* stands between you and your prize!

"AHHHH!" you scream another war cry and charge the mechanical monster, but the robot explodes before you reach it. You don't consider how weird it is for a robot to blow up on its own. You can't think about anything besides the Endgame.

The Endgame.

The Endgame.

Blinding light hits you when you step into the volcano. You squint, then gasp. That shadow you just saw? There are more of them. Like, a lot more. They're all fighting each other inside a massive, multistory arena.

You join the brawl and quickly discover that these shadows are stronger than the one outside. And they don't like being pushed around. Once you start fighting, more shadows join.

When they start piling on, you get woozy. You fight off the dizziness, then spring free of the pile. Back on your feet, you notice something's wrong. It's darker in here. The woozy feeling returns, even stronger this time.

The shadows are coming back to finish the job, but they look different now. They all have the same outline—it looks like a sleek spacesuit. That's a familiar shape, isn't it? Your world is spinning now. The darkness is really closing in.

That outline. It's . . . you. Is the Endgame filled with hundreds of versions of yourself?

When that thought crosses your mind, the creepy man and grid flash in front of your vision. This time, there's an eye symbol in the top-right corner of the grid. Then, everything goes dark for good.

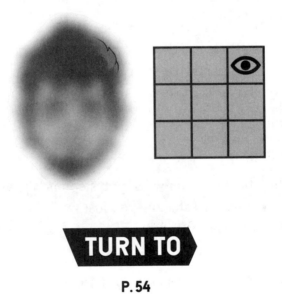

TURN TO

P. 54

BONZAI RIPS A TREE FROM THE GROUND and carries it into the forest. Great! He must have a plan. You fall in line behind him. Three minutes and eight trees later, you realize that there is no plan. Bonzai just likes uprooting trees. "Where are we going?" you ask.

"GRRR!"

You check the map in your visor. Dead center of the forest. It sure feels like you've been walking longer than that. Two minutes later, you check the map again. You haven't moved. Uh-oh. You panic and start sprinting. You run past Bonzai, then keep going until you're out of breath. You look at your map. Still in the center of the forest. You turn around. Bonzai is right there.

"WE'RE TRAPPED!" you scream to Bonzai. "TRAPPED FOR GOOD! WE HAVEN'T MOVED AN INCH!" Bonzai shakes his head. You shake Bonzai. "DO SOMETHING!"

Bonzai sets you on one of the trees he's plucked and lifts it above the top of the forest. You can see your team a mere 100 feet away. Chaz waves. Then, Bonzai flings you back to the rest of the squad. If you're not on board with his hobby, he doesn't want you.

T

❗ ACHIEVEMENT UNLOCKED
COOL HOBBY, BRO

RETURN TO CHECKPOINT ON P. 141

YOU FLEX YOUR CHEST and concentrate on the tingle. Then, you watch the next few seconds play out over and over and over: In the reality where you electrocute the cube, there will be a giant flash followed by an explosion. All of the cubes will disintegrate. You won't survive the blast.

"You see what happens, don't you?" the Builder asks.

"I don't care." (That's a lie. You care quite a bit.)

"These cubes represent my greatest achievement. They're mankind's greatest achievement. They must not be destroyed."

Pay attention.

Liz's words from the mall echo through your mind. You breathe deeply, then refocus on the upcoming moments. There are the cubes. There's the electricity. There's the flash.

Pause.

What's that? In the nanosecond between the flash and the explosion, you catch a glimpse of another world.

You focus harder and see that there's one more possibility—a portal back to the real world that cracks open for a split second before the cubes explode.

"We can make it!" you tell the Builder. "Before the explosion, there's a . . ."

That's as far as you get before the Builder launches himself at you.

The Builder has seen the future too. He knows he can't stop you. But he also knows that this is his last chance to protect the cubes.

You fire your electric pulse, zapping every cube in the room. Then, you toss the two cubes you're holding high over your head. It's a juggling move that would make Chaz proud. The cubes' collision results in a flash of bright, white energy. There's the portal.

You save yourself by reaching for the portal. The Builder dooms himself by reaching for his precious cubes.

ZZZZZZAAAAAAAP!

Everything goes dark.

Blink.

Blink.

You can't believe it. You're back in your bedroom! You touch your head, and instead of clinking Alpha's helmet, you feel your hair! Ha! You did it! Everything's back to normal!

Well, almost normal.

You start flipping through this book, and it's just a regular book at first. But when you reach the end, different realities start streaming past your head. There's one where you throw the book away. Another where you burn it. There's even a reality where you sell it.

The scenes don't stop when you turn your attention from the book. You look up and see what happens when you choose to go downstairs and what happens when you stay in your room. You watch different versions of yourself trying to explain this adventure to your parents. The scenes keep coming one after another until they overwhelm your brain. You fall asleep from exhaustion.

Many hours later, you wake up with a start. There's only one thing on your mind now.

Liz.

Who was she, really? What happened to her?

You close your eyes and focus on the scene at the mall.

It's much harder to do this in your head now. Your ability is fading fast. You pay attention to the symbols on her Q-pad while she's jumping.

Her finger is covering one of the symbols, but maybe you still have enough to find her.

Find the page with the grid that looks like this one.

TURN TO

```
R  ●  X
◆  4  C
J  Q  A
```

"HOW EXACTLY DID YOU GET HERE?" you ask Miss Eleanor.

"I never leave any of my darlings behind. We stick together like horseflies on a hound." She leans closer. "Don't we?"

There's that threatening tone again. "Totally. I'm all about teamwork. Um, this place is wild, isn't it?"

Miss Eleanor looks confused. "It's nothin' special. Just a box."

"But it keeps changing."

Miss Eleanor shakes her head like she still doesn't understand, then plops down on an office chair that immediately turns into a throne.

"How do we get out of here?" you ask.

"We wait for help."

"Maybe help is behind this door." You reach for the door, which causes Miss Eleanor to leap to her feet.

"Don't touch that," she says with fire in her eyes.

L ❗ ACHIEVEMENT UNLOCKED
HORSEFLIES ON A HOUND
RETURN TO CHECKPOINT ON P. 94

A LIGHT FLICKERS ON IN THE MANSION. You creep toward the front door to investigate.

"You know no one is in there, right?" Dark Pulse asks.

You nearly jump out of your skin. "Shhhhh!"

Dark Pulse rolls her eyes and opens the door. Naturally, it doesn't simply swing open. This is a haunted mansion, after all. It creeeeeeaaaaaaks open. You creep forward a few steps into the mansion, then hear a *THUD* from upstairs. You jump, but Dark Pulse jumps even higher.

Dark Pulse refuses to admit that she was scared. "That was nothing."

Tap-tap-tap-CHUNK.

Three hollow, metal taps echo through the house, then something sounds like it breaks. Dark Pulse turns to walk back out of the house, but you grab her arm. "Help me figure out what's going on." You march upstairs to investigate.

THUD!

You knock over an urn at the top of the stairs. Then, you enter the first bedroom. There's a large, metal pipe sticking out of the floor. What's that? You tap it three times, then it snaps in half with a *CHUNK*.

You freeze. Three taps and a chunk. That's the sound you heard earlier. Wait, was the thud from that urn the same thud you heard when you walked into the mansion? How could that be?

You decide to test the theory. You pick a lamp off a nightstand and smash it against the ground.

CRASH! Tinkle-tinkle-tinkle.

Ha! If the sounds had been coming from you, you definitely would have heard the lamp crash earlier. You march downstairs, a little less scared of the haunted mansion. "Let's head out before . . ."

CRASH! Tinkle-tinkle-tinkle.

You stop breathing. *You* are the ghost haunting this mansion.

ACHIEVEMENT UNLOCKED

THE GHOST

RETURN TO CHECKPOINT ON P. 141

ONE TABLE CATCHES YOUR ATTENTION because it can't quite figure out what it wants to be. Half of it looks like the coffee table at your dentist's office with magazines strewn all over it, and the other half looks like it came from the Tower of London. The two sides switch, then transform into a Waffle House table.

You bend over to get a better look and feel static on your face. That leads to the familiar woozy feeling. You reach down to steady yourself on the table and get zapped with a huge jolt of electricity.

You stumble back and give Miss Eleanor a "did you see that?!" look, but she seems unimpressed. She probably wants you to shock yourself to death. Not going to happen. You're getting through that door.

❗ ACHIEVEMENT UNLOCKED

WAFFLE HOUSE

RETURN TO CHECKPOINT ON P. 94

AS SOON AS the last symbol clicks into place, you feel light-headed. Everything gets fuzzy. You struggle to hang on to consciousness. Then, suddenly, the world snaps back into focus.

You're back in the previous room. Miss Eleanor is no longer there. In her place is a man at a desk who is absolutely freaking out.

"No, no, no!" the man cries while holding his head and rocking back and forth. He's got giant blueprints spread out in front of him. You recognize the amusement park. And the airport. Taped to the wall is a giant artist rendering of the Endgame volcano. "Please, just a little more time!" he yells to no one in particular.

This is the Builder, isn't it? You slink back into the shadows.

The man bends over the blueprints and grips the table so hard that his arms start trembling. Then, his whole body trembles.

The trembling doesn't look like normal shaking—it's more like video game glitching. Suddenly, his arms snap back to his head, and he's back in the same state he was when you found him. "No, no, no!" he repeats. Colors and shapes start swirling over the Endgame picture.

Now, you're starting to doubt that this is the Builder. He doesn't seem like he's in charge.

The glitching is getting worse. He starts disappearing and reappearing all over the room. One time, he's hunched over blueprints, another time he's celebrating some victory, and yet another time, he's playing chess by himself. Through all this, you've yet to see his face.

Finally, he turns around.

When he does, you feel a sudden pain in your head. Then, dizziness. The world goes dark. You recognize the face, of course. Most of it is blurry, but you still know it's the creepy guy. Next to his face is a grid with a star in the right-center spot.

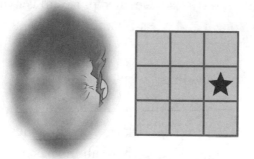

TURN TO

P.54

GRIM ISLAND, just so we're all clear, is an island for supervillain criminals floating in the middle of a lava ocean. Yes, it does have things supervillains love, like an amusement park and a creepy forest, but it is essentially a prison. So, it may surprise you to learn that the inescapable floating prison island has a floating prison of its own. Azkaar Asylum is an airship prison hovering 100 feet above Grim Island. It is for the worst of the worst criminals. It is inescapable.

When you land at Azkaar Asylum, the first thing you notice is that everyone has escaped. Which makes sense, because if there's one thing that comic books have taught us, it's that anything that's supposed to be inescapable, impenetrable, or invincible is the one thing that will get escaped, penetrated, and vincibled.

The second thing you notice is a hologram countdown floating over the asylum. It's currently at 58 seconds. Your team seems to be taking this countdown seriously. As soon as she lands, Dark Pulse uses her pulse power to speed inside the prison. Bonzai and Miss Eleanor fall in line next, followed by Chaz.

"Where are we going?" you ask Chaz.

"Property vault," Chaz says between huffs and puffs. "When villains get locked up in Azkaar Asylum, their property gets stored in a big vault. That's where all the best weapons are."

You spot another clock inside the asylum. Thirty-five seconds. Thirty-four.

"And why are we running?"

"The asylum is wired to explode if prisoners escape," Chaz explains. "We've got 30 seconds left. Most players don't land here because that's not enough time to raid the vault."

"Then why are we here?!"

"Because you suggested it!"

You reach the vault with nine seconds left. Whoa. You've hit the motherlode. There's a golden Stink from the Sky to your left and a golden Bazooka Bowler to your right. Plus, weapons you've never seen before. Your visor labels a Samurai Shrink Ray, a Blizzard Blaster, and something called a Last Day on Earth. The ultimate prize, however, is hanging from the ceiling. It's the robot that always shows up right before you reach the Endgame.

Up close, you can see that it's not technically a robot. It's a mech suit.

(You know what a mech suit is, don't you? It's one of those things that the action hero climbs inside to fight Godzilla in the movies. Although the suit's not big enough to take down the big monster, it does eventually earn Godzilla's respect, allowing the hero to team up with the great beast in the movie's final battle to defeat the ultimate evil. Anyway, one of those things.)

"That's XL," Chaz says when he sees where you're looking. "Impossible to reach before the vault explodes. Nobody has ever gotten it."

Four seconds. Time to bail. Dark Pulse is struggling to open a hatch. "THIS IS WHY I NEVER LAND HERE!" she complains.

Two seconds. One second.

Then, just before the place blows up, something remarkable happens: XL falls from the ceiling and squashes your entire team.

Whoa. How did that happen?

You drop at Azkaar Asylum again and pay closer attention once you reach the vault. With three seconds left on the countdown, XL's head hatch closes. At two seconds, his eyes turn red. At one second, the mech drops from the ceiling. No one ever enters the hatch.

How could that be? Who's controlling the mech? And why does it always explode just before the Endgame? If you're going to find out, you'll need to stay alive past the asylum explosion.

That proves to be a tougher task than you'd expected.

It takes you hundreds of tries to figure out the 16-step sequence of events you need to raid the vault and safely reach the ground. Here's just a sampling of those steps:

Step 1: Yell, "Miss Eleanor is a white-livered, yellow-bellied, chicken-hearted poltroon!" behind her back and blame Dark Pulse so you can clear some space to work.

Step 4: Spray something called "Goner Goo" around the perimeter of the vault so the floor falls all the way down to Grim Island when XL lands on it.

Step 9: After crashing from the floating asylum down to the island, change Miss Eleanor back into a Southern belle by offering her a purple petunia.

Step 15: Sacrifice Chaz by swapping his juggling balls for super grenades. Yes, this does have the unfortunate side effect of blowing up Chaz, but it also distracts XL for two seconds, giving you just enough time to execute the all-important Step 16.

Step 16: XL is now charging at your squad. To keep them safe, you're going to have to throw yourself at Miss Eleanor, anger Bonzai by kicking him in the nose, and dodge an already peeved Dark Pulse's karate chop. You'll need to time your diving twist kick down to the nanosecond to pull it all off.

CONTROLLER-BREAKING CHALLENGE

To get a sense of how difficult the timing is here, close this book, then open directly to page 135. If you're off by even one page, try again. Like many video games famous for making people break their controllers in frustration, this challenge is honestly not a ton of fun. Try it a few times, then turn to page 135 the normal way if you get frustrated. We won't tell.

TURN TO

P. 135

YOU SET DOWN THE JELLY and load Dark Pulse on your back. "Forgetting something?" she asks when the Peanut Boom starts beeping again.

"It's my only choice." You start climbing the ladder. "I can't see how I do this without leaving the Jelly alone with something, and I trust a bomb more than I trust you."

"That's sad."

"It really is."

Dark Pulse lets you climb a few more rungs, then casually says, "You know, Peanut Boom only has a 10-second timer."

You look down to see that the red light is blinking super fast now. "Why didn't you tell me?!"

"You wouldn't have trusted me if I had."

BOOM!

❶ ACHIEVEMENT UNLOCKED
NEVER TRUST A BOMB
RETURN TO CHECKPOINT ON P. 137

THERE IT IS! The key is right next to Miss Eleanor's foot. How are you going to get it? Any violence or sudden movement is out of the question. If you're not fast enough or strong enough, it's crocodile time. No, you have to sweet-talk her. But how do you sweet-talk a sweet-talker?

"Miss Eleanor," you try. "What is your favorite pie?"

"Huckleberry," she says without hesitation.

"Oh! Uh, great. And what is your favorite song?"

"'Yankee Doodle Dandy.'"

She's not lowering her guard. You've got to switch gears. "My, Miss Eleanor, are those lace flowers on your dress?"

"They're petunias!" Miss Eleanor blushes while doing a little bow.

"How daring!" you say. "I've never seen lace petunias before! Roses, sure, but never petunias."

"When I saw them in the latest issue of *Gurdey's*, I just had to have them!" Miss Eleanor spins.

Yes! Perfect. You need her to spin again.

"And the ruffles!" you exclaim. "I've never seen such!" Miss Eleanor giggles and twirls again to show off the ruffles. You cheer long and hard, encouraging her to spin and spin. When her back is turned, you snag the key.

Miss Eleanor suddenly stops twirling. She looks distraught. "Why did you stop clapping?"

"Oh! Uh, no reason," you stammer.

"What?" Miss Eleanor is suddenly alarmed. She steps toward you in panic. "Is something wrong with my dress?"

She doesn't know about the key? Maybe you can use this to your advantage. "I mean, there's nothing wrong if the lace is supposed to be dragging on the ground like that."

"WHAT?!"

Miss Eleanor is now consumed entirely with trying to see the back of her dress, presenting the perfect opportunity to . . .

"ROOOAAAR!"

Well, nearly a perfect opportunity. She sees what you're doing just as you turn the key. You dive into the mysterious room, then lock the door before Miss Eleanor slams into it at full speed.

You breathe a sigh of relief, then turn around to explore the secrets this room has to offer.

Hmm.

You're a bit puzzled. The only thing in this closet-sized room is a grid on the floor. It's filled in with nine symbols, but they're not the symbols you've collected so far. What happens when you enter them into your Q-pad?

Find the page with this exact grid on top to reach the next section.

TURN TO

CHAZ RACES PAST YOU into the shack and jumps on the bed. "Wheee! Can we move this house into a tree? Please? It would make the perfect best buddies tree house!"

This would actually make the perfect murder house. Rusty nails are scattered across the floor, a chain is keeping the freezer closed, and Chaz will probably get tetanus from springs sticking out of the bed. This is the dumpiest dump you've ever seen, and you recently visited an actual dump.

Chaz hops off the bed and opens a cabinet. "Leftovers!" he yells. "They've got leftovers!" He dips his finger into a jar and licks it. "Sour! Very sour!" He drops the jar, spilling white goo all over the floor.

You roll your eyes and turn to leave before Chaz breaks anything else. That's when you spot one last door.

"Don't open that!" Chaz yells when you reach for the knob.

Now, you're definitely going to open it. You throw open the door to find . . . yourself? You're just looking at a mirror.

"DON'T GO IN!" Chaz launches himself at you. Of course, that's the opposite thing you should do when you're trying to pull someone backward, but this is Chaz we're talking about. He tackles both of you into the mirror.

The funny thing is, this isn't actually a mirror. It's the same cabin; the only difference is everything is now moving in reverse. You watch yourself look inside the room, then close the door. A second Chaz is standing in front of the fridge. "Taht nepo t'nod!" he yells. Then, the shattered jar on the floor reassembles itself and zips back up into Chaz's hands.

You look back at the Chaz who tackled you through the door. All the color has drained from his face. "We need to leave," he says.

You push past him and jog outside. Everything's moving backward out here too. You watch your team strap on parachutes, then fly into the air.

CLINK!

Chaz wraps the chain from the freezer around you. "So sorry to do this," he says as he drags you back into the cabin. You struggle and dig in your heels, but Chaz doesn't slow.

Then, just as Chaz reaches the mystery door, you try one last move. You close your eyes, focus on the tingle in your chest, and squeeze.

ZING!

You zap Chaz just as he steps through the doorway. He drops the chain and stumbles backward.

WHOOSH!

A wave of energy ripples through the doorway. Chaz reaches for you again, but he can't get his hand past the doorway.

You realize that Chaz just went backward through the reverse door at the five-minute mark of this game. That's the same time he talks gibberish and dances in reverse at the dump. Did this moment somehow cause that one?

No time to figure that out now. You wave goodbye and run back outside.

Out here, the buildings are even simpler polygons than you remember. Trees are disappearing. You've traveled all the way back to the creation of Creepy Country. You hear a noise behind the shack and run to check it out.

Oof!

When you round the corner, you slam into someone. It's a man dressed entirely in black. A blueprint falls from his hands. This is the Builder! It has to be! You reach for the blueprint, but he dives on it first.

"Who are you?" you ask.

The man doesn't look up. Instead, he fumbles with a Q-pad.

"Wait!" You rush to flip him over and get a better look at his face. Just as you do, he enters a code into the Q-pad.

ZAP!

Everything goes black. The only face you see is the creepy guy. Next, you see an *H* in the top-left side of the grid.

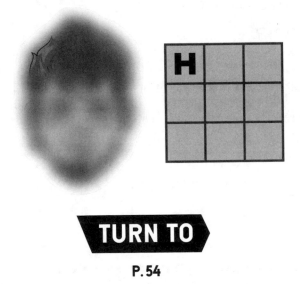

TURN TO

P. 54

NOW THAT XL IS ON THE GROUND, it's time to go on the offensive. "Let it rip!" you yell to your team.

Boy, do they let it rip. Both at XL and you. Here is the collection of sounds that assaults your ears when your team unloads:

CRASH! BRANG! AWOOOOGA! ZWOOOOOOOWITY!

Guess what? None of it does any good. Your teammates' weapons can't hurt you, and they don't seem to affect XL either.

After they're done, XL does a push-up and springs from the ground, stronger than ever. He balls up two fists, rubs them together like those paddles doctors use to restart peoples' hearts, then launches himself at your team and shocks you all.

Time to start over. You need better weapons. The good news is there's a whole vault of better weapons to choose from. Over the next 132 attempts, you try everything in the vault. Highlights include:

Tennis Trainer: A gun that spits an endless barrage of tennis balls. Instead of hurting XL, it appears to help his backhand.

Fire Hose: It's not what you're thinking. This is a hose that shoots actual fire.

Beehive: Bees do not like being used as weapons. They share their displeasure by stinging your hand over and over.

Cheesecake Factory: A conveyor belt whips cheesecake after cheesecake at XL. They all look very expensive.

Nothing works. But wait! What if you combine weapons?!

You combine the Cheesecake Factory with a Firework Finale to make exploding cakes. You mix a Bazooka Bowler with the Porcupine Popper for spiky cannonballs.

Then, you discover the Squirrel Squadron.

The Squirrel Squadron is a crossbow that shoots well-trained flying squirrels at enemies. Outfitting Squirrel Squadron with a rocket will allow the crossbow to launch something much bigger than a squirrel. So, you pick up a Hammer of Horrors, then get Bonzai to launch you at XL.

CONTROLLER-BREAKING CHALLENGE

You've got to hit XL squarely in the eye to cause damage. To understand how challenging that is, close your eyes and put your pinkie on this page. If you touch the letter *I*, turn to page 146. Feel free to skip this challenge if it feels like we're just being difficult to make the book feel longer.

TURN TO

P. 146

GRIM ISLAND'S ENERGY PLANT is a giant tower perched over a dam. If this setting feels familiar, it's because this is exactly the type of place all movie villains try to sabotage on their path to world domination.

Your team lands just outside the plant and loads up on weapons. Another team is doing the same. Bonzai spots the squad, growls, and chases them toward the facility. Someday, you'd love to have a team meeting where you can kindly remind your squad that they don't have to engage with every team they see.

Chaz follows Bonzai with a "WOOHOO!" before stumbling into rushing water and getting sucked over the dam. It's four against five now, but your team follows the enemy squad into the facility anyway.

An eerie green glow lights the tower. Water rushes below the grates. Above you are several stories of pipes and catwalks, but no enemies.

"WHERE ARE THEY?!" you shout over the sound of rushing water.

Miss Eleanor starts to answer, but a shark falls from above and swallows her whole.

They've got a Shark Cannon! There! You point at a Santa with tattoos two stories above you. Santa waves back and aims. Bonzai leaps toward him and gets a face full of shark.

Now, it's two on five. The other team has you trapped. It's like shooting fish in a barrel (in this case, quite literally firing actual fish inside of an actual barrel). But instead of going for you, the enemies scramble up to the next platform, strap on jet packs, and lift off.

One look below, and you see why. Apparently, some villain couldn't resist sabotaging the Grim Island energy plant. The water is rising fast.

"How do we get out of here?!" you shout to Dark Pulse.

Dark Pulse is much less interested in the "we" part of that sentence than the "get out of here" part. You spot her scrambling up to the jet pack platform. "Wait!" you yell.

WHOOSH!

Dark Pulse, of course, does not wait. Instead, she rockets all the way to the top of the tower, where the enemy team is escaping through a hatch. Tattoo Santa fires his final shark at her before leaving the tower. Dark Pulse spins to avoid the shark but loses control of the jet pack. She smacks every single walkway on her way back down to you.

"Unnnnnng," Dark Pulse moans and writhes. "I can't walk on this leg."

You want to leave Dark Pulse here. You really should leave Dark Pulse here. But seeing her like this reminds you that you're a better person than that. You can't abandon her now.

Water is rising quickly. There's got to be some other way out. You climb to the next level and find another hatch, but this one is blocked by rubble. There's also a purple backpack that looks like some sort of power-up. You strap on the backpack and climb down to Dark Pulse. Wow, this backpack is heavy.

"OK, there's a hatch, but . . ." You squint at Dark Pulse. She's got a backpack that looks exactly like yours except it's brown instead of purple. "What are you wearing?"

"Peanut Boom," Dark Pulse says. "You've got the Jelly. The brown one's the bomb, the purple one is the detonator."

Perfect! This is exactly what you need. If you get Dark Pulse and the two backpacks up to the next level, you can blow open the hatch and escape. You'll have to make separate trips for everything because Dark Pulse and the backpacks are too heavy to carry at the same time. Of course, you can't leave Dark Pulse anywhere near the Jelly backpack or she'll double-cross you and activate the bomb the first chance she gets. You lean in to explain your plan over rushing water.

"I don't trust you with the detonator, so I'll come back . . ."

Beep! Beep! Beep!

The Peanut Boom backpack starts flashing. Dark Pulse pushes you away.

"If the backpacks get too close to each other, they'll explode. Anti-safety feature."

"*ANTI*-safety?!"

"Standard villain stuff."

Great. Now, you've got to somehow get Dark Pulse, the Peanut Boom, and Jelly up the ladder without leaving the Jelly by itself with either Dark Pulse or the Peanut Boom. Remember, you can only carry one item at a time. What do you move first?

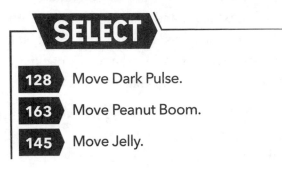

SELECT

128 Move Dark Pulse.

163 Move Peanut Boom.

145 Move Jelly.

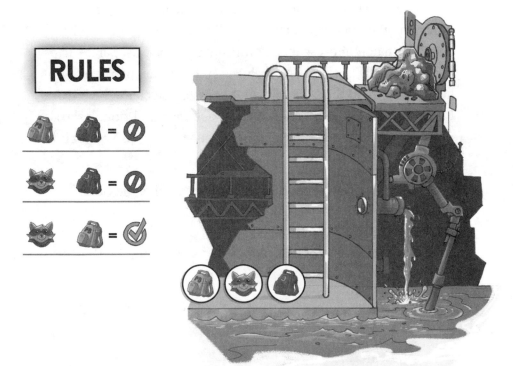

PRACTICALLY EVERY VIDEO GAME has a spooky section. Maybe the lighting is a little lower, the trees have no leaves, or a few surprise bats fly in front of your face. The thing about all that is . . . it's not actually scary. That's why you're not worried about Creepy Country.

You should have worried.

It's so scary. From the moment you drop, you feel the urge to run and hide. At first, you're not sure why—Grim Island doesn't add much to the standard spooky video game formula. It's got all the staples: a menacing violin soundtrack, a night sky even though it's daytime everywhere else on the island, and elaborate jack-o'-lanterns. So why is this so much scarier than every other video game you've ever played?

Eventually, you realize that the world feels scarier because you're actually living in it. It's the difference between watching someone walk through a haunted house on YouTube and actually living inside a house that's haunted by real ghosts.

Also, this area feels unfinished. Like, the graphics settings here seem to be turned to "low." There's a bit of glitching to your right. That doesn't make you feel good about your safety.

There's something else too. "Why are we the only ones here?" you ask.

Dark Pulse looks around. "See anything worth getting?"

While every other area of Grim Island has been filled with loot, you can't find the glow of a single weapon anywhere.

"Plus, people disappear around here all the time," Chaz says. "Whole squads will get wiped out for no reason."

Dark Pulse starts leading the team toward the Endgame, but you stop her. If weird things are going on here, you'd better investigate. Where do you want to explore first?

SELECT

101 Cemetery.

113 Eternal forest.

119 Haunted mansion.

131 Old cabin.

THE MIND MELD is a tall throne with a glass dome suspended over it. Is this your superweapon? You check out a nearby electric panel to see if you can make something happen.

Complete the circuit by rotating only three pieces. Put the numbers from the pieces you choose in order from left to right to get your next page number. The first five words of the correct page are, "Once the electric panel crackles."

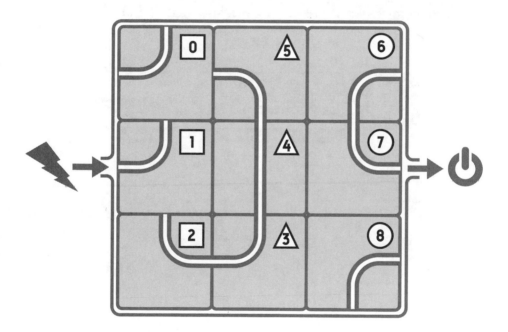

TURN TO P. _____ _____ _____
□ △ ○

YOU'RE GOING TO FIGHT THE BUILDER. Even though you can't move. This does not seem like a good idea. You ignore the searing pain in your head and use all your strength to ball your left hand into a fist.

The Builder chuckles when he sees the fist. It's a classic bad guy chuckle and your first clue that this fight isn't going to end the way you hope it will.

"I see that you've figured out your purpose here," the Builder says. "In order to claim victory over other realities, I need to first claim victory over you. I take no pleasure in doing this."

N ⓘ ACHIEVEMENT UNLOCKED
CLASSIC BAD GUY CHUCKLE
RETURN TO CHECKPOINT ON P. 166

NOW, YOU'VE GOT the Jelly on top of the ladder with Dark Pulse and Peanut Boom at the bottom.

"You know, if you weren't the way you are, this would be a lot easier!" you yell to Dark Pulse.

She winks. Now, you've got a tough decision to make. Do you move Dark Pulse up next or the Peanut Boom?

SELECT

153 Dark Pulse.

162 Peanut Boom.

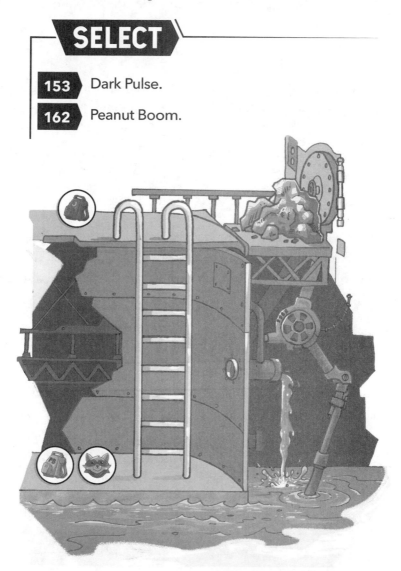

ON THE FIFTEENTH TRY, you finally land a hammer blow to XL's eye.

Tink!

You did it! You cracked the eye! Its red light even flickers a little! XL then plucks you out of the air and eats you.

So that's it. All that work for one little *tink*. What do you do now? Give up?

Never.

Around attempt 607, this became personal for you. You are going to defeat this mech if it's the last thing you do. Maybe you can lure it into lava. Is there a way to trap it inside the vault? Perhaps you can become friends with it. You spend 38 attempts just trying to give XL gifts.

Nothing works.

After a thousand tries, you land on one final conclusion: You can't defeat XL. If you're going to win this battle, you need to stop the fight from happening in the first place. You need to get inside that robot first.

CONTROLLER-BREAKING CHALLENGE

You've got to move fast if you want to reach XL before the mystery opponent. To understand how fast, read the rest of this section in under two minutes. If you read fast enough, turn to page 158. If not, try again. Keep trying until you realize that nothing's stopping you from turning to page 158 even without completing the challenge.

This turns out to be your most difficult challenge yet. While previous challenges required split-second timing and precise aim, this is pure concentration. One lapse, even for a moment, and you blow up before reaching XL.

Make no mistake: You do blow up. Many times, in fact. After a few dozen attempts, you start understanding why Chaz said no one ever goes for XL. It truly feels impossible. But then, you discover a shortcut to the vault. Next, you find a pair of spring-loaded boots. Maybe this isn't so impossible after all.

Each time you cycle through the asylum, you learn something new that helps you move a little faster. Most hacks only save a quarter of a second, but that time adds up. You're getting closer and closer to XL with each pass. Your head is also feeling worse and worse.

You start getting that icky sensation you recognize from playing video games too long. Your head heats up, and your brain feels like it's slogging through mud. You start seeing a human-shaped blur near XL's hatch. Random colors and shapes play across your vision. Wouldn't it feel nice to take it easy for this next attempt?

NO.

You're so close that you keep bumping your head on XL's hatch just as it closes. You can't give up. Not now. You shake your head to clear the cobwebs and squint. You're going to make this speed run count.

You jump out of the plane the instant it enters Azkaar Asylum airspace and make your body as aerodynamic as possible before pulling out your parachute a foot from the ground. You hold on to Dark Pulse as she pulse speeds into the asylum, then slingshot off of her into a vent that will get you to the vault faster.

You drop from the vent directly onto spring shoes, then bounce into a mess of computer cables. You flex your chest to electrify the cables, which launches you up to the ceiling. If you bounce off the ceiling at just the right angle, you should land inside XL's cockpit. Except it never works. Even on the tries when you get the angle right, you can't seem to jump hard enough.

This time is different. This time, you focus on the last remaining electric tingles in your chest and move them to your feet.

ZZZING!

Electrifying your spring shoes does the trick. You tumble inside XL's cockpit just as the hatch closes.

TURN TO

P. 158

WHEN YOU POINT OUT the three trees, Dark Pulse activates her superpower. She whips out a pair of nunchucks then pulses toward the trees with superspeed. "AHHH!" you hear one second later from Tree #1. Then a similar scream comes as Dark Pulse takes out the second sniper. Finally, you hear a ding and check your counter. Only one other squad left!

You step out from behind the rock to congratulate Dark Pulse. That's when the last squad surrounds your team. Four ugly witches toting golden weapons smirk at each other. This will be the easiest victory of their lives.

You feel that tingle in your chest again. You squeeze your eyes closed, hold out your hands, and go for it.

ZAAAP!

A full-fledged lightning storm shoots from your body and zaps every last enemy.

BRAAANNNG!

A foghorn sounds. You're the last squad! On your first try! You step through the trees to find a stone bridge over a lava moat. Across the bridge stands the Endgame. A portal filled with blue light has cracked open at the bottom of the volcano.

You run across the bridge to get a head start on the Endgame.

"OOF!"

Suddenly, you find yourself on the ground. It feels like you've been tackled by an NFL linebacker even though no one else is on the bridge. You struggle to your feet, and it happens again.

"OOF!"

There's a blow to the ribs. This time, you stay down and try to get your bearings. You notice the scenery around you ripple. Is someone using an invisibility suit? "Help," you moan.

Dark Pulse steps over you without a word. Miss Eleanor leans down. "What's the matter, hun?"

Someone pins your hands to the ground. You can see the ripple of the invisibility suit clearer than ever now. "ARE YOU NOT SEEING THIS?!"

Miss Eleanor looks genuinely confused. So are you. Aren't you the last squad? Where did this other person come from? You try focusing on your chest, but the electricity needs time to recharge. Before the Invisible Man can finish you, the world dims.

BOOM! BOOM!

Something has moved in front of the sun.

"It can't be!" Miss Eleanor shrieks. "It's—it's XL!"

A robot half the size of the volcano has stepped between your team and the Endgame. The Invisible Man lets you go now that you both have a common enemy.

XL the robot sprouts 200 different cannons from its arms and chest. While most of the weapons on Grim Island feel pretty silly, these are deadly serious. The giant bot points all 200 weapons directly at your team, then . . .

KABOOOOM!

. . . Self-destructs before it can shoot you. What was that all about?

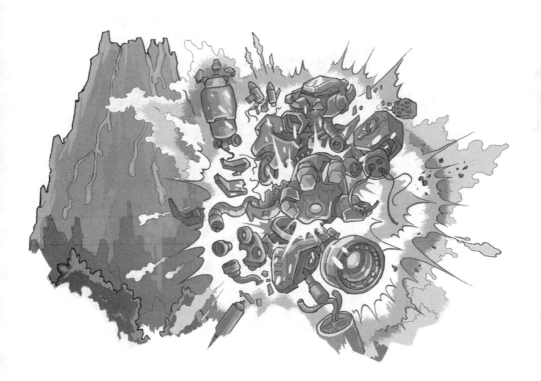

Dark Pulse smirks and spreads her arms. "Welcome to the Endgame! See you on the other side." She runs through the portal. Miss Eleanor clenches her fist, changes into a crocodile, then follows Dark Pulse.

This is it. You step into the light and brace yourself.

As soon as you set foot into the portal, darkness envelops you. You try pushing past it, but you feel like you're fighting the ocean. Your vision gets blurry, and your head starts spinning. "Dark Pulse?" you yell. "Miss Eleanor?!"

You spot two things before the darkness overtakes you: The first is a square with a circle in the middle. The second is a face. Most of the face is blurry, but the eyes—the creepy eyes—are very much in focus.

Finally, everything disappears.

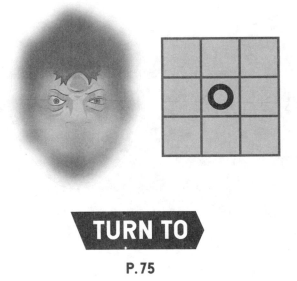

TURN TO

P. 75

A	4	R
C	◆	6
4	M	★

OK, SO YOU'VE MOVED Dark Pulse and Jelly to the top of the ladder. Just one more item left. But here's where it gets tricky. You see, you can't just leave Dark Pulse and the Jelly together. Dark Pulse will absolutely betray you if you do. You've got to take one of them back down. Which is it?

SELECT

145 Dark Pulse.

157 Jelly.

THE SOLUTION IS SIMPLE: Use your former team's programming against them. "Chaz!" you yell. "Let's see that juggling routine you've been working on!"

Chaz's scowl evaporates, and he produces three juggling balls from his pocket.

"Not now!" Miss Eleanor hisses.

That's something Chaz can't compute. It's always juggling time. He throws the balls high into the air, shuffles left, then steps on Miss Eleanor's dress. She turns into a crocodile and eats him. Next, you stick out your tongue at Bonzai, which causes him to charge and trample poor Miss Eleanor.

Your last step is getting Dark Pulse to betray her team. When her back is turned, you roll a Hen Grenade toward her. Then, you watch her eyes light up when she spots an opportunity to kill you and betray Bonzai in the process. She picks up the explosive egg, then looks confused. Where's the grenade's pin?

BOOM!

You've already pulled the pin. The apartment falls on top of Dark Pulse and Bonzai, but you've seen the exact spot you need to stand to remain safe.

Once the building collapses, you spot the Builder sprinting toward the jungle. You run after him but get intercepted by XL. Not now! The possibilities start flying.

In one reality, you run around the island trying every weapon that might scratch XL's armor. You blast the mech with a Mama Llama Bomba, then lead him into a giant mousetrap, then punch him with a spring-loaded fist. XL's armor remains unscratched. .

Maybe you can distract him. You bust out Chaz-inspired dance moves. You try a hypnotizing ray. You even cobble together a beautiful girl robot in hopes that XL will fall in love. Unfortunately, his heart is made of steel.

Can you outrun XL? You cannot.

Finally, you see your one opportunity to take down XL.

Find the page that contains this grid.

ONCE THE ELECTRIC PANEL crackles to life, you hop in the throne.

ZAP!

The glass dome lowers and starts shooting sparks at you. It doesn't kill you, though (at least not yet). Instead, everything goes dark, and a familiar sight fills your vision: the map of Grim Island. Then, just like you remember from when those snipers had you pinned in the jungle, symbols start appearing on the map. You're a blue triangle, your teammates are green squares, and all the enemies are red dots.

"What do you see?" Dark Pulse asks.

You open your mouth to answer, but then something weird happens. The triangle splits off into another triangle. And then another. Then, triangles pop up all over the map. There are even a few clustered in one spot on the lava sea. Wait, is this saying that you're in all these places at the same time? That can't be.

You start feeling dizzy. The harder you struggle to piece together the mystery, the dizzier you feel. Finally, the map gets replaced by the creepy guy's face. Then, there's a new symbol. It's a *W* in the top center-spot of the grid.

TURN TO

P. 54

GREAT. NOW THE PEANUT BOOM AND JELLY are at the bottom level together with Dark Pulse up top. As soon as the two backpacks get close to each other, Peanut Boom starts beeping again. You've got to move one of these bags up the ladder. Which do you choose? Hurry up. You only have a few seconds.

SELECT

170 Peanut Boom.

153 Jelly.

THE ONLY THINGS INSIDE XL'S COCKPIT are a small window, lever, captain's chair, and seat belt. (The seat belt is an unexpected, yet welcome safety feature for Grim Island). Oddly missing is any sort of control system.

You hold on tight as XL releases from the ceiling, squashes your crew, then drops all the way down toward Grim Island. The big mech starts stomping toward the Endgame, taking out every team in its path. You stomp on a squad of land mermaids. XL kicks a few full-grown mutant ninja turtles. A zebra with a unicorn horn shoots a rocket, which XL snags out of the air and tosses back. You're not controlling any of it.

Wait a second, why isn't anyone else in here with you? Who was inside XL all those other times you saw him? If the answer is no one, then does that mean . . .

You're coming to a realization, but every time you get close, your head starts swimming. The Grim Island map takes over your vision as if your own brain is trying to distract you. You look out the window to clear your head and find that you've reached the volcano. XL turns around to face the bridge. You see two shadow figures fighting each other. That's when everything clicks.

The person inside of XL has been you all along.

By trying to stop the robot, you actually became the one who unleashed it. You can't think about it too hard because it makes your brain hurt, but that's the only conclusion that makes sense.

If that's true, then you're also the only one who can stop XL.

You rip open your seat and find a control panel. You'd like to short-circuit it with your electrical power, but you still need to recharge. Maybe you can sabotage XL some other way. This next part will require precision.

CONTROLLER-BREAKING CHALLENGE

Understand the level of precision needed here by turning this page using just your breath. Can you do it? If not, turn the page anyway. You're running out of time.

TURN TO

P. 160

X	4	C
I	●	U
8	N	Z

YOUR VISION IS A BLURRED MESS. A thousand thoughts from a thousand different loops all collide in your head. You feel helpless. What happens if you fail?

You start operating on instinct. Move this wire here, remove that spark plug over there. Have you done this before?

One more button, then—

Beep!

Did you do it?

Beep!

Your vision clears enough to see out the window again. One of the shadows is running toward you.

Beep!

You brace yourself for the boom, but before XL explodes, the scene outside the window changes. First, it goes black, then it turns into the creepy face. Finally, you see the number one in the left-center spot of the grid.

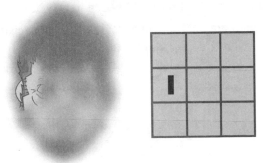

TURN TO

P.54

THE DUMP! OF COURSE! There was so much junk there! You start exploring the dump with the intensity of a garbage rat.

There's so much to explore. Whoever made this game did an amazing job with the dump. It is, without question, the most detailed dump to ever grace a video game. Here are some of the things you find in your many, many visits to the dump:

- A SpongeBob square bowling ball

- One thousand crafts that parents threw away when kids weren't looking

- Fidget spinners

- Every single Beanie Baby

- A toy that makes creepy sounds because its battery is almost dead

- Kale

After a thousand cycles at the dump, you start slowing down. At first, you think it's just because you're getting tired, but it's more than that. Your feet feel like they're sticking to the ground. Everyone else is slowing too. You notice stuttering. It's getting harder to think. Strange colors and patterns cloud your vision. Eventually, objects start melting together. This can't be good.

T > ❗ ACHIEVEMENT UNLOCKED
SPONGEBOB SQUAREBALL >

RETURN TO CHECKPOINT ON P. 73

V	Q	E
R	T	Z
●	3	4

NOT A BAD CHOICE. Except the Peanut Boom is beeping again. Peanut Boom and Jelly are now together at the top with Dark Pulse at the bottom. You've got to move one of the backpacks down, quick. Which do you move?

SELECT

145 Peanut Boom.

164 Jelly.

MAYBE YOU CAN TRUST DARK PULSE alone with the Jelly. "If I bring the Peanut Boom up first, you're not going to use the Jelly to detonate it, would you?"

"Of course not!"

"Because I'll be holding it."

"Right."

"And that would be a really mean thing to do."

"Wouldn't dream of it."

You give Dark Pulse a stern look to let her know you're serious, then strap the Peanut Boom to your back. Five rungs up the ladder, it starts beeping.

You look down to see that Dark Pulse has opened the Jelly bag and pressed the detonator. "SERIOUSLY!"

She shrugs. "Couldn't help myself."

BOOM!

⓵ ACHIEVEMENT UNLOCKED
WOULDN'T DREAM OF IT
RETURN TO CHECKPOINT ON P. 137

OK, NOW DARK PULSE and the Jelly are back down together on the lower level. Time's running out. Dark Pulse's paws are getting wet. You'd feel a lot worse about this had the fox not just double-crossed you for the tenth time.

Now that Dark Pulse and the Jelly are together on the lower level, which do you bring up?

SELECT

170 Dark Pulse.

162 Jelly.

THIS MAP DOESN'T APPEAR to be the current version of Grim Island. Can you learn anything by studying it?

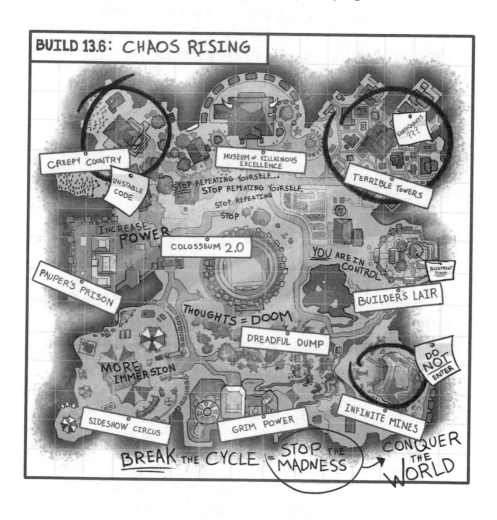

BUILD 13.6: CHAOS RISING

CREEPY COUNTRY

UNSTABLE CODE

MUSEUM of VILLAINOUS EXCELLENCE

EARTHQUAKES ??.?

TERRIBLE TOWERS

STOP REPEATING YOURSELF...
STOP REPEATING YOURSELF.
STOP REPEATING
STOP

INCREASE POWER

COLOSSEUM 2.0

YOU ARE IN CONTROL

BLUEPRINT ROOM

PAUPER'S PRISON

BUILDER'S LAIR

THOUGHTS = DOOM

DREADFUL DUMP

MORE IMMERSION

DO NOT ENTER

SIDESHOW CIRCUS

GRIM POWER

INFINITE MINES

BREAK THE CYCLE = STOP THE MADNESS

CONQUER THE WORLD

E

🅾 ACHIEVEMENT UNLOCKED

WHAT A MESS

RETURN TO CHECKPOINT ON P. 94

YOU ENTER ALL NINE SYMBOLS into your Q-pad with trembling hands. This Builder guy seems like a scary dude. What will he do when he sees you? Maybe you can sneak up on him. When you enter the final symbol, your head gets fuzzy again. You feel like you're floating, then flying.

BZZZT!

A jolt of electricity strikes your head. That flying sensation you were enjoying a moment ago turns to falling. You get a splitting headache. The farther you fall, the more intense your headache gets. Finally, you stop.

"Who are you?" a gruff voice asks.

Your head hurts so much that you can't even open your eyes, let alone answer.

"The Endgame," the voice says. "You beat the Endgame, didn't you?" Then, there's a low cackle. "Welcome to the real Endgame, Alpha."

You muster enough strength to crack open your eyes. All you see is a swirling kaleidoscope of colors and shapes. That makes your head hurt so bad that you scream.

"I'm sure you have many questions," the voice says. "I'll gladly answer them while you adjust. First, allow me to introduce myself. You can call me the Builder. This will not be a face-to-face meeting because nobody gets to see my face."

The Builder's behind you. You summon all your strength to turn toward him. You can't move a muscle.

"Second, I must clear up some confusion. Yes, you technically won Grim Island's Endgame, but that wasn't *the* Endgame. That comes in a few moments."

Why does he keep saying that you won the Endgame? That never happened.

"So why are you here?" the Builder asks. "One word: consequences. Every choice we make carries consequences. Simple decisions determine the course of your day: Do you choose left or right? Actions or words? Generosity or deceit, kindness or murder?"

You don't love that he included "murder" in that list.

"The problem with humans is that we don't know the consequences of our choices until it's too late to change. But what if we could see those consequences earlier? What if we knew exactly what would happen *before* we made the choice? Wouldn't that help us make better choices?"

Sure. It could also help someone take over the world, which is where you suspect the Builder is going with this.

"I recently obtained Bionosoft technology, but not to simply enter video games. I'm not a child. Instead, I saw the potential for the virtual to control the physical. By superpowering Bionosoft's reality mode with quantum computers, I built a device that let me bend reality back on itself. A do-over machine, if you will. Set a checkpoint, then return to that point over and over until you understand the consequences of every decision."

He's describing the Q-pad. You clutch the device close to your body to keep it hidden.

"But that's too slow. I retooled the system to let me experience all sorts of realities at once. I tried it first with chess. Seeing every possibility allowed me to play five moves ahead. Then I tried more complex scenarios. What if real people got involved? Could the technology keep up?"

All this talk about reality is making your head hurt even more.

"The tech turned out to be good but not perfect. Big events from one possible reality would bleed into others. I'd sometimes see versions of myself as shadows. My brain would play along until it saw through the illusion, then it would give up."

OK, now this is something you can relate to. The technology he's describing could explain how releasing XL one time would unleash him across every loop or how the Endgame could be full of shadow versions of yourself. The realities were all "bleeding" into each other.

"I could glimpse possible realities, but I could never hold on to them long enough to make them 'real,'" the Builder continues. "That wasn't good enough. I needed to choose my own reality with my own brain. That's where Grim Island comes from. It's not a game; it's a test."

The Builder stops for a moment to let the implication sink in. You're the test subject.

"Step one: Create an environment so convincing that test subjects believe they are Alpha. The more someone buys into the game, the deeper they'll get before their brain sees through the illusion. I took great care in crafting the locations, enemies, and especially squadmates. Alpha's teammates couldn't feel like props. Thanks to Bionosoft's artificial intelligence modules, these characters only needed a single goal and personality trait to talk and act like real people."

That's why Dark Pulse couldn't stop betraying you, and Chaz felt the need to befriend everything with eyeballs. They were simple characters programmed with basic impulses.

"Step two: Get the test subject to the Endgame across multiple realities. The game had to feel challenging enough to keep subjects interested, while pushing as many variations of the same person as possible toward the Endgame."

That checks out too. As long as you fought baddies and stuck with your babysitters, er, teammates, you generally made it to the Endgame.

"Step three: Let the real battle begin. Not the silly battle royale on Grim Island, but the fight among Alphas inside the volcano. Put enough realities together, and one will win. And look here—" the Builder gets close to your ear again. "One has won."

He's wrong, of course. You didn't get here by winning the Endgame. So, what's really going on?

"You're the One. You're going to teach me how to make one reality win over all the others. You're going to help me write the future. This is the Endgame."

Not if you can help it. What's your next move?

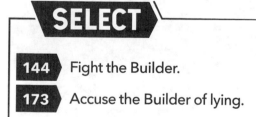

SELECT

144 Fight the Builder.

173 Accuse the Builder of lying.

DARK PULSE AND THE PEANUT BOOM are together on the top level. The fox raises an eyebrow at you when she sees how high the water is rising. "Almost there?"

You look back and realize that you are! All you have to do is go back and retrieve the Jelly, and you've made it!

TURN TO

P.171

THE JELLY BACKPACK is half-covered in water, and the shark that swallowed Miss Eleanor is just about to eat it. You snatch the backpack away from the shark and lug it up the ladder. When you reach the top, Dark Pulse smirks at you. "Need my help yet?"

You shake your head and push the Peanut Boom into place. It's heavier than you remember. You're using all your strength to push it. The water is getting closer. As you push, you hear a noise.

Beep! Beep! Beep!

"What are you doing?!" you ask.

Dark Pulse smiles. "Double-crossing you."

You are completely flabbergasted. "But why?!"

"Because that's what I do."

Beep-beep-beep!

"No, but seriously, why wouldn't you just wait until I pushed it into place?"

"What's the fun in that?"

"WE BOTH GET TO LIVE!"

You turn to push the bomb again, but then you shake your head. There's something more important that you need to do. You stomp over to Dark Pulse. "You understand that you probably doomed yourself by double-crossing me, right? So why did you do it?!"

Dark Pulse smirks again. You feel like screaming, but instead, you study her eyes for an answer. Maybe a hint of motivation or regret? Nope. There's nothing except pure joy in that simple act of betrayal. At that moment, you realize that Dark Pulse doesn't have any goal besides betraying people. But why?

Beepbeepbeep!

The Peanut Boom is about to blow, but it doesn't matter. The dizzy headache has returned. Before the water, shark, or explosion can get you, Dark Pulse's face is replaced by the creepy man's. The last thing you see is the number eight in the bottom-center section of the grid.

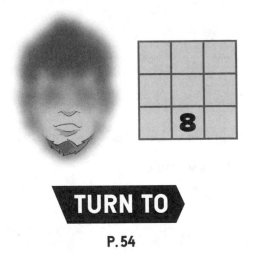

TURN TO

P.54

YOU FIGHT THROUGH THE HEADACHE to croak two words: "You're lying."

"The technology exists whether you believe it or not," the Builder replies.

"No, you're lying about the test. I'm not the test subject. You are."

The Builder chuckles like you're a little kid who just said something cute. Still, you continue. "You didn't build Grim Island for anyone but yourself. You wanted to win the Endgame because you thought that would give you the ultimate superpower: choosing your own reality."

This is a bold theory that you don't entirely believe yourself, even though you're the one saying it. But here's the thing: The Builder keeps insisting that you're here because you won the Endgame. You don't understand why he would believe that unless it's how he arrived here himself.

You squeeze your eyes closed to focus on the words you're about to say rather than the overwhelming pain in your head. "You won the Endgame, but that didn't give you the power you thought it would. I've seen what happens when you try too many times. The game starts glitching. You see colors. Shapes." You point to the kaleidoscope wall. "You get this. Beating the Endgame didn't give you superpowers. It broke the system and trapped you inside this prison."

The Builder's not chuckling anymore. Instead, he remains quiet for so long that you suspect he may have left. Finally, he says, "It's not a prison. It's the final test."

"You're wrong."

"I won the Endgame," he growls. "You won the Endgame. If I defeat you, then I'll have ultimate power. I'm sure of it."

"Killing me won't do anything."

"It will!"

"It won't because I never won the Endgame!" That silences the Builder. "I found you on my own."

Wow, that felt great! You wish you could see the Builder's face right now. He's probably gawking at you like a big doofus. Instead, the Builder snatches the Q-pad out of your hand. "Where did you get this?"

"A friend."

The Builder gets quiet while he studies the Q-pad, then says, "You have coordinates for this location. That's impossible."

"I told you, I found them. I traveled to your reality by paying attention to clues all over the island. Not winning a fight."

More silence.

"Of course," the Builder finally whispers. "I don't know why I couldn't see it before." He's not talking to you anymore. He's talking to himself. "Choosing a reality isn't about picking a winner. It's about seeing things from every angle. It's not about getting sucked in. It's about zooming out."

You're not sure what that means, but you have a sinking feeling that the Builder just made a breakthrough.

"You're right." The Builder's talking to you again. "There were no other test subjects. I wanted the power all to myself, so I didn't tell anyone about this project. That means no one was here to save me when I got trapped. I never thought I'd escape."

He leans close. "I don't know who you are or how you got into the game, but I must thank you. You're a true hero."

"Wait!" you shout.

You can hear the Builder tapping on the Q-pad. "Do you know about the history function on this? I can go everywhere you've been. See everything you've seen. Once I examine Grim Island from every angle, I'll have ultimate power."

Your head hurts so bad. "But I did see the island from every angle! Where's my ultimate power?!"

"So close," the Builder says. "You're just missing one angle."

"Which one?!"

The Builder pats your shoulder. "It's not so bad here. You get used to the pain. Eventually, you'll even open your eyes. Might I recommend the kaleidoscope show? A million ruined realities all crashing into each other. If you stare long enough, you'll feel it meld to your face. It's neat."

With that, the Builder disappears.

You're alone. Worse than that, you're certain that you've unleashed evil upon the world. You've got to escape, but you can barely open your eyes. When you finally crack them open, you're greeted by a swirling sea of colors and shapes. You feel like throwing up but force yourself to keep your eyes open.

Eventually, a single shape starts to form out of the chaos. You concentrate on that shape, then gasp. It's a face.

TURN TO

P. 176

How to See the Face

1. Bring the book all the way to your face. Touch the center of the pattern with your nose.

2. With the book held close to your face, focus past the image as if the book didn't exist. Pretend you're looking at something in the distance. The pattern should be blurry.

3. Hold that focus while slowly pulling the book away from your face until an outline starts to appear within the pattern.

4. Once you see the outline, hold the book still and maintain your focus. Give your eyes time to adjust. An image of a face should slowly form.

5. Don't worry if you can't see the face! Most people need at least a few tries. Be patient, take it slow, and move the book back and forth until you start seeing something.

6. Your eyes will want to focus on the page, but you must fight that urge in order to see the picture. Relax your eyes and maintain your focus on that imaginary point in the distance so the pattern remains blurry. If your eyes ever refocus on the page, you'll need to start over at the first step.

7. Once you've seen the face (or if you're just ready to move on), turn to the next page.

TURN TO

P. 178

THAT'S IT! THE BUILDER'S FACE!

But that's not the face you've been seeing around the island, is it? You close your eyes and try putting all the blurry images together.

Suddenly, it clicks. That face you've been seeing? It's not a separate person. It's the Builder! He's just upside down!

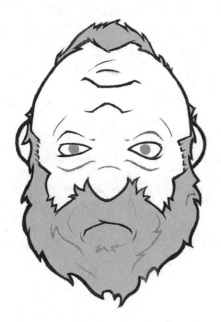

Your mind is racing. If the face was upside down, then maybe the grid was too.

Return to page 55 and flip the book upside down. This upside-down version of the grid is the correct one. Find the page with this new grid in the header to reach the next area. Redrawing this new version of the grid on a separate piece of paper might make your search easier.

TURN TO

P. 55 AND ROTATE BOOK

YOU'VE RETURNED TO the locked closet, although it's not a closet anymore. The back wall has opened to reveal a table holding six glowing, blue cubes. You pick up a cube in each hand just before the Builder figures out where you are and follows you into the closet.

ZAP!

This is the first time in four million realities that the Builder has looked nervous. "Those are the most powerful objects on the planet," he warns.

"I'm going to destroy them."

"They're running the game. Destroy the cubes, and you destroy yourself."

"I know."

He steps closer. "Keep one and gain unlimited power."

Two realities appear in front of your face. Which do you choose?

51 Keep the cube.

114 Destroy the cube.

```
Z  ▲  4
6  T  ■
G  3  X
```

YOU FOCUS ON THOSE EIGHT SYMBOLS until your brain hurts. Finally, a ninth symbol clicks into place, and you transport from your bed into a cold, metal room.

What is this? Some sort of industrial freezer? And why does it smell like sardines?

The only thing in this freezer is a single sheet of paper. You pick it up.

Wow, you did pay attention! Congratulations. I know you must have a lot of questions about who I am. About what I'm doing. I'd like to show you. To unlock your final adventure, find every ending in this book. Each ending has a secret letter that you can fill in on the next page. Once you find all the letters, you'll uncover a secret code that you can enter at escapefromavideogame.com. Good luck.

-LIZ

Secret Message

Fill in the secret letter that goes with each achievement. When you enter all the letters, you'll spell a phrase. Enter that phrase at escapefromavideogame.com to unlock a secret story.

___ SPONGEBOB SQUAREBALL

___ THE TROLLEY PROBLEM

___ THE GHOST

___ NEVER TRUST A BOMB

___ HORSEFLIES ON A HOUND

___ NO-GOOD VARMINTS

___ GALAXY BRAIN

___ NATURE'S FIRST VILLAIN

___ 818

___ CAN'T DODGE A TROLLEY

___ NOT FOR LONG

___ BEEFY BRAWLERS

___ WOULDN'T DREAM OF IT

___ NEW TEAM

___ AGREE TO DISAGREE

___ RIP ALPHA

___ CLASSIC BAD GUY CHUCKLE

___ KONAMI CODE

___ "FUN" HOUSE

___ WAFFLE HOUSE

___ COOL HOBBY, BRO

___ BULL IN A BOX

___ WHAT A MESS

___ WORSE THAN THE ELECTRIC CHAIR

___ COLLECTIBLES

___ SUPER STINKER

___ WORLD-CLASS CLINGERS

___ LOLLYGAGGING

___ CROAK

___ GARBAGE MONSTER

VISIT ESCAPEFROMAVIDEOGAME.COM
TO UNLOCK YOUR ADVENTURE.

WHEN YOU HIT "NO," the text changes. "Fine. Reshelve this book in its correct location to return home."

Return home? You look up to discover that you've somehow transported to an unfamiliar library. "Where am I?" you ask a librarian.

The librarian slides you a brochure entitled *Amherst College Library: Birthplace of the Dewey Decimal System*. "Would you like a souvenir photo in front of the Dewey Decimal mural?!" he asks in the most excited whisper possible.

You turn to see a floor-to-ceiling portrait of a stern, bearded man next to a bunch of numbers. "Who's that?"

The librarian squints. "Is this an 818?"

"A what?"

"A JOKE! EIGHT HUNDRED EIGHTEEN IS THE DEWEY DECIMAL NUMBER FOR JOKE BOOKS!" The librarian regains his composure before continuing. "That is the father of modern librarianship, Melvil Dewey, and you will show some respect."

"Um, sorry? I just need to shelve this book."

The librarian studies the binding for a moment before dismissing you. "This isn't ours. It's a Dewey Decimal number."

"But you just said . . ."

"We switched to the Library of Congress system in 1974."

This is going to be a very long day.

ACHIEVEMENT UNLOCKED
818

RETURN TO CHECKPOINT ON P. 11

Hints and Solutions

Puzzles

P. 27

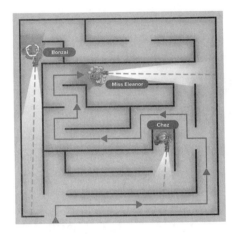

P. 40–41

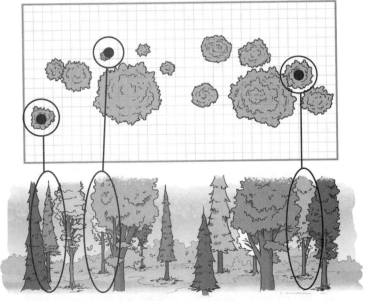

P. 50

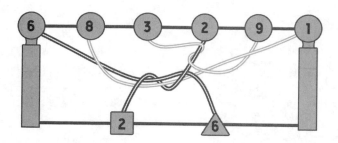

P. 70-71

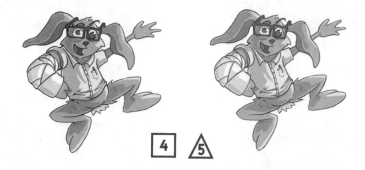

4 5

P. 94

P. 140

STEP 1. **TURN TO** P. 145

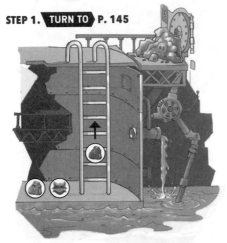

STEP 2. **TURN TO** P. 153

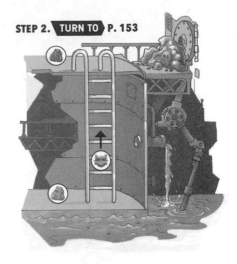

STEP 3. **TURN TO** P. 159

STEP 4. **TURN TO** P. 170

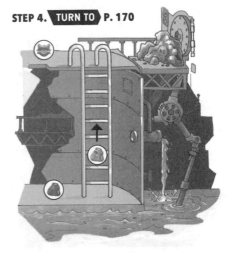

P. 143

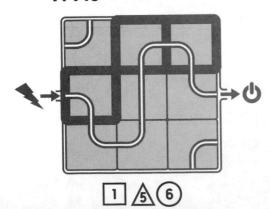

P. 177

Grids

P. 55

H	W	👁
I	O	★
X	8	I

TURN TO P. 166

P. 63

8	I	6
D	N	V
★	U	K

TURN TO P. 154

P. 109

8	H	O
■	X	●
W	M	I

ROTATE GRID 180°

I	W	M
●	X	■
O	H	8

TURN TO P. 180

P. 117

Z	▲	4
6	T	■
G	3	X

TURN TO P. 181

P. 130

8	H	O
■	X	●
W	M	I

TURN TO P. 122

P.155

V	B	4
G	H	E
X	C	T

TURN TO P. 106

P.179

H	W	👁
I	O	★
X	8	I

ROTATE GRID 180°

I	8	X
★	O	I
👁	M	H

TURN TO P. 60

About the Author

DUSTIN BRADY

Dustin Brady lives in Cleveland, Ohio, with his wife, Deserae; dog, Nugget; and kids. He has spent a good chunk of his life getting crushed over and over in *Super Smash Bros.* by his brother Jesse. You can learn what he's working on next at dustinbradybooks.com and e-mail him at dustin@dustinbradybooks.com.

JESSE BRADY

Jesse Brady is a professional illustrator and animator who lives in Pensacola, Florida. His wife, April, is an awesome illustrator too! When he was a kid, Jesse loved drawing pictures of his favorite video games, and he spent lots of time crushing his brother Dustin in *Super Smash Bros.* over and over again. You can see some of Jesse's best work at jessebradyart.com, and you can e-mail him at jessebradyart@gmail.com.

Look for these books!

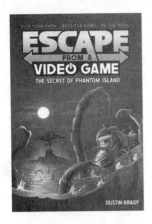

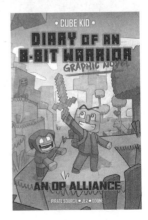